About the Author

Claire was born near Ipswich in Suffolk. She went on to
read Agriculture at Leeds University and has stayed in
North Yorkshire working with sheep and horses.

For Mummy XX

Claire F. Smith

FOUR TALES

AUSTIN MACAULEY PUBLISHERS™
LONDON • CAMBRIDGE • NEW YORK • SHARJAH

A CIP catalogue record for this title is available from the British Library.

ISBN 9781398418035 (Paperback)
ISBN 9781398418042 (ePub e-book)

www.austinmacauley.com

First Published 2021
Austin Macauley Publishers Ltd
1 Canada Square
Canary Wharf
London
E14 5AA

Contents

Frisbee 9

Taste the Rain 46

Life Choice 59

Monster In the Wood 89

FRISBEE

O F COURSE HE had always wanted a son, but as he held his new daughter in his arms he felt an overwhelming love. Still sticky with birth fluids he took in her red and screwed up face, the dark shock of hair, the tiny perfection of her hands. He looked across at his wife, her hair matted with sweat. She was at once the biggest mess he'd ever seen her and at her most beautiful. "Well done you," he said. She beamed in response. Just for a tiny wee second she worried that he wouldn't love their daughter so often had he talked of their having a son. But she could see the pride in his eyes. And who could not love the bundle of life that was Elizabeth Jane Symcox?

Jenny soon took Elizabeth, Ellie, home. She could barely walk so sore were her stitches and as for sitting down! So it was a relief that Ellie was such an easy child. She fed well, slept well and gurgled happily while she was awake. As soon as she could smile it seemed to be all she ever did, holding her arms out in glee to hug her doting parents.

She was a proper girly girl. She tucked her dolls into their pram and loved dressing up, especially if this meant shuffling along in a pair of Mummy's old shoes. She would sit on Daddy's knee while he played the piano, her tiny hands resting on his broad rough paws as they travelled over the keys. It would be how she learned to play. Geoff Symcox was a self-made man. He had started out as a mechanic, then had had his own back street garage and now owned a main dealership. Never afraid of hard work he had grafted long hours to establish his reputation of reliability and trustworthiness. Consequently 'his girls' wanted for nothing, their home was a smart detached out-of-town residence with a mature garden and a small paddock. A local gardener came once a week to cut the lawns and tend to the beds but Jo Symcox took a keen interest in the garden, the planting in the borders and the large vegetable plot. The paddock was home to sheep from a nearby farm through the summer. Jo loved to take Ellie into the garden and help the little girl with her own projects; she grew sweet peas. Put in her own special seed potato. Anything as long as her clothes stayed clear of mud. Ellie much preferred her ballet classes, she dreamed of being a swan in 'Swan Lake' and having her first pointe shoes.

Oh, and her first day at school! How sweet she looked in her uniform! A pleated crimson and blue kilt, light blue polo shirt and crimson sweatshirt with its embroidered oak tree on the left breast for Oaktree Primary. Her long, wavy light brown hair was gathered into bunches either side of her head. Geoff was as proud as punch to take his daughter to school in his Land Rover Discovery, a tear in his eye as Ellie ran into the schoolyard.

Jo and Geoff then welcomed a new arrival. When Jo first told Geoff she was pregnant he wouldn't have minded another daughter, but here was a bouncy baby boy. He came into the world a full two pounds heavier than his 'big' sister weighing in at 8lb 8oz. Thomas Edward was very different from his sister with always a frown on his little face. He cried for milk, guzzled it and cried with wind. He cried in the night he cried through the day. Ellie was at first enchanted by him but as he screamed louder than ever if she so much as touched him she soon went back to her dolls and her dancing. As he grew he was sturdy, healthy and handsome. He smiled more and frowned less but, by heck, he was naughty. Like the time he found the kitchen scissors and cut all the hair off every one of Ellie's dolls. Ellie was mortified, poor Fifi! And Angelina! Scalped! Jo placated her with a pair of rollerblades; surely she was getting too old for dolls now? He would have got up to more badness at his sister's expense, like cutting off *her* hair, but Ellie had mastered the art of delivering a Chinese burn. If she wasn't careful he would be nasty with her, pulling hair and biting. If she said anything to Mummy he was so good at turning things round. Oh, butter wouldn't melt! As big sister she always got the blame. She learned to block him out of her bedroom with her dressing table.

And so Thomas took to playing by himself in the garden. There were swings and a climbing frame but he preferred pulling up the vegetables and stripping the plants of their leaves. When Jo tried to reason with him, saying he was damaging the plants, he threw tantrums, running at his mother and swinging his fists at her. Restraining him made him worse and Jo took to bribing him with sweets and ice cream.

By the time he attended school Ellie had gone up to juniors. I know she will have been delighted to go to a different 'branch' of Oaktree. In many ways Thomas was a model pupil, that is to say, he was good at his lessons and was clearly very bright. But, well, he wasn't much of a mixer and, unlike his sister, had few friends, never seeking the company of others. Once or twice he was downright aggressive; he stuck a pencil in Wayne Smith's ear-blood and enraged parents all over the shop, and virtually scalped Pippa Edmonds pulling out hair having followed her into the girls' toilets. He was banned from playing football at break times as he always went for the player rather than the ball. But, hey! Boys will be boys!

I think the first really bad thing he did was with the rabbit. Ellie had pestered for a pet for her birthday. Let's be honest, she could have had anything within reason but she really wanted a rabbit. An English Spotted doe bunny was duly purchased and it was the sweetest thing. Ellie adored Dottie and she kept the rabbit in her bedroom where it had a litter tray, bowl of water and a bed. Dottie never used the bed as she was in Ellie's. At first, Jo had a meltdown about a rabbit indoors but it really was very clean... During the day Dottie had a run and hutch on the lawn. Ellie would go and fetch Dottie out as soon as she got back from school and Dottie might sit on her lap indoors or nibble the lawn outside as Ellie performed handstands and cartwheels down the long garden. Thomas took against Dottie; he thought it smelly and stupid. One evening, when Ellie had gone to friends for a sleepover, he went to the kitchen and fetched out the big scissors with orange handles. He balanced the scissors in his small hands. How shiny the blades! How sharp! He checked around to make sure Mummy was busy elsewhere then crept down the garden. Pretty Dottie bobbited right up to him so it was easy to pick her up and carry her and the scissors to the bottom of the garden. Thomas decided he would start by cutting off Dottie's ears. 'Snick!' went the scissors and off came an ear. Poor Dottie screamed and screamed as a rabbit will. And kick? Oh, yes, as hard as she could. Thomas was quite unprepared for this and soon began to lose his grip as the terrified rabbit bucked and wriggled for all she was worth. In the struggle, Thomas stabbed down hard with the point of the scissors tearing the velvet skin of Dottie's shoulder. Dottie's paws found purchase on the grass and she streaked off down the garden, a blur of white at 30mph, over the compost heap and under the leylandii bordering the garden. Here she crouched, heart racing, remaining ear flat to her head. Alerted by the cries of the rabbit and scenting blood, the neighbour's black Labrador, Storm, came a-running and a-sniffing down next door's garden. He fixed on the rabbit in no time. She saw him too, but dithered just a fraction too long, even as she ran Storm scooped her up in his jaws. Dottie went limp as if playing dead and Storm pressed her to the floor and pinned her with his paw before picking her up once more. He was just getting her comfy in his mouth. Then head high with the weight of the rabbit he trotted off up the garden to deliver Dottie to his master, his mouth so soft on Dottie, his task to retrieve, not to kill. Only Mrs Rogers was in so Storm made do with her. He deposited Dottie at her feet in the kitchen and once again Dottie shot off this time parking herself under the Welsh dresser, well out of reach. Mrs Rogers phoned Jo who coaxed Dottie from under the dresser with carrot. Mrs Rogers was quite clear that Storm had only found Dottie, he wouldn't harm a fly. Jo wasn't going to argue, she just wanted to take the poor animal to the vet. Thomas would have to come with her. Where was the lad?

Thomas meanwhile had been getting his story straight. He hid the scissors under a stone behind the shed, stuffed his blood-stained T-shirt as far down the wheelie bin as he could reach without falling in while balancing on the wall. He dragged some neatly tied bin bags over the top. He heard Mummy call. He got in with his version of events straight away; "Mummy, I was playing with Dottie and she ran under the hedge and that big black dog grabbed her and bit her and ripped her ear off and ran away with her before I could get her back…"

"It's a naughty dog, darling, let's get poor Dottie to the vet."

Despite the vet saying the injury was unlikely to be done by a dog, Jo and Geoff believed Thomas. When Geoff went round to the Rogers' they said Storm *would not bite*, but they paid the vet bill anyway, it wasn't worth falling out with good neighbours over. And they put a new fence up.

Yes, Thomas had learned a lot from the rabbit saga, that if you want to torture individuals they are likely to scream and shout about it, that even small things need suitable restraint, that it's a good idea to have a fair alibi to get away with it. That his parents believed, or at least wanted to believe, that he wouldn't hurt Dottie was a big plus, but Ellie had him bang to rights. Her garden search didn't throw up any evidence; that didn't matter, she could see the smug satisfaction on Thomas' face. She knew how cruel he could be and was also aware that he was growing big and strong. She asked for a lock on her bedroom door.

* * *

Time passed, as it will. Ellie went up to the local comprehensive and Thomas was up to junior school. Ellie's social calendar was jam-packed: she still did her ballet and they were busy preparing for a performance of *The Nutcracker*. Then she was in the netball team all summer and the hockey team in winter, plenty of evening matches! With her sunny personality, she had oodles of friends, lots of stopovers. It was like she was even more popular for being an ordinary-looking girl; anyway, her smile would light the room. Often she would still play piano with Dad, both of them squashed onto the piano stool.

It was hoped that Thomas had grown out of the phase of wanting to hurt things and, indeed, the incident with Dottie, who had since passed away from natural causes, was all but forgotten. Not by Ellie, of course; leopards and spots and all that. And how right she was. Ever since seeing that Indiana Jones film, *Temple of Doom*, he had been obsessed with the removal of a beating heart from a body. Imagine it! Talk about holding life in your hands! He announced that he was going to be a heart surgeon and started to amass as many books as he could on anatomy and especially hearts. Geoff and Jo thought this very commendable indeed. What an intelligent boy he was!

Though Thomas had aptitude for sport he showed no interest in being in anyone's team. He was never invited anywhere, nor did he ever ask for anyone to stay. Then, out of the blue, he announced he wanted a puppy – and why shouldn't a lad have a dog? In the end it was decided to buy a family dog, one for everyone to walk and play with but wouldn't drop hair everywhere. They settled on a Cocka-poo. Actually, Jo and Ellie went to pick him up, a cute ball of ochre fur, good-natured and full of beans. What would they call him? Thomas was mortified when his suggestions of Fang and Ripper were dismissed and they finally settled on Bob. Ellie tried not to become attached but who could resist this happy, pretty puppy? She would try to brush him and he would try and eat the brush. An endless game. Jo loved trip-ping over him in the kitchen (no, really) and that she could spend hours coiffing his poodle locks. Geoff couldn't wait to take him for walks. Strangely, Thomas had less time for him. Why wouldn't it do what it was told? All it did was nip and chew. Sometimes he had to get rough with it, twist its legs, pull its tail, just to get it to listen. Very quickly Bob learned to steer clear of Thomas, his tail tucked between his legs as he scooted away when Thomas came in the room.

As Bob grew, Thomas realised he was going to have to get the dog on side if he wanted to really get stuck into it. He started giving Bob secret goodies, pieces of cheese, biscuits. At first, Bob was wary, but a dog is a dog and biscuit is biscuit. Jo noticed that Thomas was bonding with their new pet much better now and was pleased. Meanwhile, Thomas was exploring means of restraint. String was no good, the knots were too difficult; and he got himself into an awful mess with duct tape as it twisted and stuck where he didn't want it. No, the cable ties were the best, if you remembered to get them the right way round. He had dug out the orange-handled scissors and had acquired a serrated vegetable knife as well.

At last, an ideal day arrived. Daddy had gone to golf, dropping Ellie off at the dreadful Rosemary's on the way. Mummy was doing cleaning. She was potty about cleaning, all her hair scraped up in a scrunchie, pink rubber gloves on. She would never have a cleaner: "Not having some busybody going through my smalls..." she would say. Whatever smalls were. Plenty of time for him to deconstruct Bob, then leave his body on the back lane as if it had been hit by a car. He knew how he would spread him out, like the dead fox he had seen there. Tools tucked up his jumper, he enticed Bob to the garden shed with the promise of custard creams. Actually once the shed door was shut it was a good deal darker than he had expected. This may have altered the position of his cable ties. Certainly, the one round Bob's snout would prove to be too far back from the nose. The second and third ties held Bob's front paws together, the fourth and fifth his back. Unable to stand, Bob wriggled worm-like and whining on the tarpaulin the gardener used for lawn clippings that Thomas had spread over the floor. Thomas cracked the shed door for a bit more light.

Firstly Thomas removed the ears; they were much tougher, more cartilaginous, than Dottie's. The scissor blades became slippy with blood, which didn't help either. Then he sat on the young dog facing its backside and began chopping into his tail. More difficult still, especially as he hit the bone to begin with. By now Bob's cries had escalated into an eerie low howling, restricted as he was by the tie on his jaws. Turning round, Thomas went for the main event where he would cut along under the ribs and finally expose the heart. Concentrating hard, he made a stab with the vegetable knife, just behind the ribs high on the pup's left flank. Bob whisked his head round, as high and as hard as he could. His good nature exhausted, the growl of rage was deep in his throat. As his jaws were still restricted by the cable tie, he was unable to open them fully, but still he managed to get a good hold on Thomas' nose and bit down for all he was worth. Thomas howled with shock, Bobs' head had given him a good thump in the face and at first it felt numb, then he felt the needle teeth on his nose and his own blood flowing over his top lip. Boy, did he yelp! Then as Bob fell back to the floor, Thomas was dragged forward by the weight of Bob as he flopped back down, performing almost a complete forward roll, his little nose wrenched from Bobs' grasp. Leaving Bob where he lay, the vegetable knife stuck in his flank as a picadors' lance from a bull, Thomas ran up the garden, through the French doors into the sitting room, to Mummy, his T-shirt pressed to his nose.

"Mummy, Mummy! Bob bit me!"

Jo turned from dusting the piano to see her blood-soaked son. There were arterial blood spurt patterns over his new jeans, over his trainers, his hair. Blood all over his hands as they covered his face. "Oh. My. God!" Jo felt light-headed. Call for an ambulance. No. Take too long. In the car, now.

"Thomas, oh, my darling, what happened? Let's get you seen to."

At the hospital he was seen quickly. It's weird, but once he was all washed off he had just the injury to his nose. From all the blood they had expected worse. Relief all round. The nose was cleaned and needed one butterfly stitch. The doctor said he may have a couple of little scars. His eyes were beginning to blacken already. Panic over, Jo drove home. Geoff was staying at the club for lunch – agh, she could have done with him home. Now she would have to deal with that dog all on her own. Leaving Thomas in front of the television with some ice cream, she went to look for Bob in the garden. "Bob! Bob!" She called then listened, then, as she neared the shed Bob answered her call with a stifled "Orrawff." Why didn't he run up?

She looked round the shed door. She saw the poor, bloody dog, all tied up.

"Fuck. Shit!" Surely not? But there was no other explanation: this was the handy work of her son. She lifted the secateurs off the shed shelf and released Bob, the knife falling to the floor from his flank. Bob whined and wagged his stump, a funny grin across his face. What a relief to be rescued!

Jo's first thought was to get the dog to the vet. She ran up to the house and fetched a large towel, only to find Bob had followed her up the garden, his coat stuck with blood. I think this is why she forgot to pick up the cut-off ears and tail, she was in such a state. She wrapped Bob up in the towel and shouted to Thomas. He would have to come with her, he was too young to stay home alone. He ambled into the kitchen where Jo held Bob in her arms, completely unconcerned.

"I found him like that. He bit me when I tried to set him free," lied the boy. "Can I have pop?"

"No, we're going."

Jo wanted to pick Thomas up and shake him. How could he?

Even as she drove to the vets she wondered what she would say. "Here is the dog my son cut up." And then she remembered the ears and tail, were they still in the shed? She glanced at Bob in the rear-view mirror. How odd he looked now the softly folded ears had gone. She didn't want to look at it. Ever again. She passed the veterinary surgery and headed out of town, into the country. Her mind played over different scenarios. What Geoff would say to Thomas, to her? What about dear Ellie? She would be devastated. The more she thought about it, the more it made sense to her to lose Bob, make up some story. One thing for sure, Thomas wouldn't care. She glanced at him now in the rear-view mirror, nose bandaged, sore eyes closed in sleep. She was actually not too sure of where she was: a country road, a good distance from home. How long had she got? She would have to have time to clean up any blood before Geoff was home.

Seeing a lay-by ahead, she swerved into it. She climbed out of the car and listened: birdsong, the lazy buzz of a fly, the breeze through the trees. No one in sight either. She lifted open the boot and let Bob out of the wire mesh kennel. He half-fell, half-jumped to the floor. He was beginning to feel very stiff and sore. Quickly Jo shut the boot and shimmied back round to the driver's side door. Checking Thomas was still asleep, she got herself comfy in the driver's seat, fastened her seatbelt, indicated right and drove speedily away. She never looked back.

Bob watched the car go. He hurt. His ears and tail and ribs hurt, but most of all he was little more than a puppy left all alone goodness knows where. He set off in the direction that the car had taken, at first a steady jog, but pretty soon he was travelling with a definite cant, his vision beginning to blur. Thirsty, thirsty, trot, trot! Despite the warm summer evening he was beginning to feel cold. He never clocked the car. The driver of the Ford SUV didn't notice Bob either, as he was messing with his climate control. He felt a bump, though, checked his rear-view and saw something gingery laid on the roadside. Fox probably. Sorted the air con, drove on.

Ike was taking the back roads home as he'd had a couple of pints. Dying for a slash, he pulled the flat deck into the muddy little lay-by by Graves' wood. After relieving himself, he stood a while by the truck, taking in the cool dusk, the smell of nettle and willowherb. He dug his fags out of his pocket and flicked on his lighter. The flame caught something not far from where he stood, catching his eye. Letting the lighter burn, Ike, stooping, stalking, went to see what it was. A dog. Its eyes were what had caught the light. Yes, it was alive, but it looked bloody sick.

"Narn, son, how ist? Eh?"

The poor sod whimpered in reply.

"Reckon as you've been run down, hev ya?"

Ike took a last long drag on his fag before flicking it into the verge, popped the lighter in his pocket, then picked up the dog, laying him gently on his jacket on the passenger seat. He studied the dog awhile. It looked young, gangling and half grown. What had happened to its ears? Its tail? His missus had been pestering him for one of these cock-apoo things but they was too dear. Well now she got one. He'd take some fixing, mind. Then he remembered Haggie Annie. She was a queer fish, that was for sure, would've been burned at the stake years back. If you drove past High Moor Farm you came to three little old cottages, cute two bedroom affairs, a brick over the door of the middle one saying '1693'. Now go a little further still, right into Graves' wood and there was another little dwelling, single-storey and older still. It was enclosed by a chestnut paling fence and a carved wooden sign next to the wicket gate. "Deepwood" murmured the sign through its layer of moss and lichen. It was here Haggie Annie lived, boiling her herbs and rescuing hedgehogs. Only last week he had fixed her old van, bought a battery for it an' all and she said, she said, "I'll be doing you a favour next week." How did she know then, about the dog? Yeh, Haggie Annie would fix the dog and that would save a vet's bill. Then May could hev it.

The hour was late by the time Ike pulled up at Annie's cottage, yet there was a light showing within. He tucked the dog under his muscular arm and carried it up the path to the cottage. Even as he raised his other hand to knock Annie opened the door, much as if they were expected. Indeed, there were decoctions of willow bark, poultices containing marjoram, yarrow and aloe vera, a restorative drink with chamomile and dandelion, all laid out on the hearth.

"Come, come," she waved them in, "put the beast down near the fire." Our Annie always kept the fire in summer and winter.

Haggie Annie was a little over five feet and stick thin. Her hair was long and beautifully thick and silky, wound into a plait down her back. No one knew her age, but it was significant; her face wrinkled, yes, but the bone structure of a beauty still in evidence. And her eyes, oh those eyes! Sparkling violet. Stunning.

Her hands ran over the dog, they felt the broken humerus, the stab wound. Her fingers felt the microchip in the neck and she made a pinching movement. Without leaving a mark on the dog she now held the chip between her fingers.

Whoever had owned this animal wasn't having him back; the chip was flicked in the fire.

"Give me a few days and I'll have him right as rain."

"Fair do's," replied Ike. He didn't know about the dog but he really needed his bed.

All that night Annie tended to the pup. She fixed the leg with a splint, she dripped herb tea in his mouth to rehydrate him, his cuts and grazes were carefully bathed. They finally fell asleep together on the old leather settee before the fire.

Haggie Annie was woken by Grace singing as she walked down the cottage path, the slightly out of tune trilling of a happy child. Born tongue-tied with a harelip, Grace had had several operations to correct her deformity, but there would always be the scar on her lip, the uneven teeth, not to mention the lisp. Bullied at school for the way she looked and spoke, she had run away from home when she was but eight – well, all the way to Graves' wood with a toothbrush, an apple and £3.50. Thinking to herself she had run very far indeed, she sat on a log and cried her heart out. Here Haggie Annie found her: normally she would give anyone in the woods, child or otherwise, a wide berth, but the waves of distress emanating from Grace disturbed the peaceful ambiance of the afternoon. Ascertaining that Grace was leaving home, she took her back to Deepwood. Soon she had Grace feeding the fire and preparing vegetables for the stew; she was going to have to learn these tasks if she was to make it alone! On the pretence of collecting firewood Annie walked up to the three cottages to report the finding of Grace and maybe, she said, Grace could stay the night at the cottage. Grace stayed that night and the next. She was mesmerized by the rapport Haggie Annie had with the animals in the wood; even the deer did not run from her. Haggie saw a tall, strong child and her enthusiasm for learning all about the herbs and animals of the wood utterly delighted her. By the time Annie walked Grace back to the end cottage where she lived with her mother, Cheryl, they had become firm friends.

Cheryl worked as a secretary for High Moor Farm and was grateful of the tithe cottage, a haven after she had split from Grace's waste of space father. She found it suited her to have Grace spend time with Annie, somewhere safe to leave her daughter during school holidays while she was working. And Grace always came back in good spirits, full of tales of rescued animals, flowers and fungi. She sent Grace down with milk, bread, cheese, things Annie couldn't grow. She learned Annie was particularly thrilled with a jar of coffee – what a treat!

On one of her visits Grace came to Haggie Annie with a soft toy dog cuddled close and tears in her eyes.

"You will have to rescue him," Grace sobbed. "I bought him from the charity shop, but Mummy says he's evil. She said he bit her ankle and it's not, it's NOT true! She's going to put him in the bin!"

"Let's have a look at him then," Annie said kindly. "Look, he has a little hole in his leg. Let's get him stitched up."

"He's called Frisbee," announced Grace. Frisbee's leg was duly stitched and a bandage applied. Grace looked much happier.

"Look, he can live here on the back of the sofa," Annie said, placing the toy dog on the broad back of the chair. It was an appealing-looking thing, about a foot long with soft tan-coloured fur, legs spread akimbo and soft floppy ears. A fuzzy black nose sat largely under rather close set eyes of shiny glass, their colour changing with the light. There was no visible mouth for biting ankles! Grace seemed happy with the arrangement and went out with Annie to collect eggs from Annie's hens. Later that day, as she was leaving, Grace went to Frisbee and kissed him goodbye.

"Good dog," she cooed. "Be a good boy, see you tomorrow."

Annie thought the toy looked smug. How daft is that? She gave the thing no more thought until she went to bed. And then she plumped her pillow and folded back the checked blanket to reveal Frisbee spread as wide as his little legs would go across the bed. For a brief moment she was cross with Grace for going into her bedroom – but wait, she remembered her kissing it goodbye. Anyway, she wasn't taking it back to the living room now.

"Come on Frisbee, time for sleep." She could swear the thing wagged its short tail!

From that day Grace would often carry Frisbee round under her arm when she visited and Annie would take him to her bed at night and back to the living room during the day. It saved the dog moving itself. Yes, you could often put him down somewhere and he'd be found somewhere else. And another thing, if Annie left a plate out, like the time she had left a crust of bread and cheese rind, the plate would be licked clean. By a toy, with no mouth? The pair of them talked to Frisbee as if he was a real dog. How the little glass eyes shone, their colour deep brown, the plush fabric of his coat soft and shiny.

But back to Grace waking Annie: here she was, carrying a small bag of groceries, coming to spend the day with Annie in the long summer holiday. As she wrestled to close the gate with one hand and not drop the bag out of the other, she heard the barking. A broad smile spread across her face. A dog! Annie had got a real dog! She ran up the path to see what sort of dog it was. The little russet dog continued to bark defensively at Grace until Annie sort of, well, introduced them. Once he had given her a good sniff he decided they were friends. He was doing his very best to be playful with his leg held rigid by the splint. Frisbee must have spent the night with Annie and the young dog as now he was perched on the arm of the settee, his eyes glowing red. Reflecting the dying embers of the fire, perhaps?

"He looks a bit like Frisbee, don't he?" Grace said of the young dog. "'Cept Frisbee got ears." After tea and porridge for all, they all bounced up the lane in Annie's van to buy some proper dog food. Grace insisted on buying a toy for the dog, settling on a squeaky ball. This turned out to be a saviour for the furniture, clothing – well, everything, really, as this pup chewed whatever he could get hold of. Not Frisbee, though, oh no, the new dog behaved with him like he was a real dog, nudging the ball towards him and inviting him to play. Grace had been told that Ike was having the dog and he would give him a name, but you have to call a dog something don't you? And Grace loved to give things a name. Though Haggie Annie had carefully soaked the blood from the dog's coat, his fur was still tangled with road dust. As Grace tried to brush him she decided as he was all matted up he could be Matty, so Matty he became.

All too soon for Grace Saturday came around and Ike bought May along to pick Matty up. Grace was throwing the ball across Annie's living room and Matty was off after it, going well on the bandaged, splinted leg. Annie was trying to remain cool when Matty knocked something else over, looking forward to it being just Frisbee in the house, when Ike and May walked in. Matty immediately dropped the toy and began to bark at May. Clever dog: he remembered Ike, the deep voice, yes, but mostly his smell, the blend of cigarettes, pasties, engine oil, but these things also masked the more subtle scent that was uniquely Ike. Matty had him down as a friend.

Grace was pleased Matty had remembered Ike, it made it okay that he was going to be Ike's dog. Still, it was quiet without him. Haggie Annie started getting things back off shelves where they'd been placed out of Matty-range, Grace nattered on and on about the dog: it was Matty this and Matty that. Finally Annie, putting her hand on Grace's shoulder: "There will soon be other animals to look after, you know."

It was Cheryl who bought the kitten home. Poor little mite was found in one of the potato sheds at High Moor, eyes open, ears pricked but too young to walk without wobbling. In her lunch hour she tucked the kitten up her T-shirt which was then tucked into her jeans, a sort of cosy sling, then walked down to Haggie Annie's. There was Grace, cleaning out the chicken shed, ha! Never did chores like that at home! Although at first worried by her mothers' unusual early show, she was delighted to be presented with the little ball of fur. He was as light as a feather and she could cup him in her two hands. His eyes were smoky blue as they had not long opened, his coat a grubby white. Annie came out to inspect him and announced they would give him a feed of milk with raw egg whisked in for now, then it was another trip to the pet shop for special kitten milk and food, Cheryl left them to it.

Now this kitten was all Grace's kitten. She fed him milk out of a syringe until he was strong, then fed him milk moshed up with kitten food. He was kept in her bedroom by night and transported, by handbag, to wherever she went by day. Soon he began to outgrow the handbag and, being too wriggly and lively to carry, would follow Grace down to Annie's. Boy, did he sulk if he was left at home while Grace went to a school friend's. Grace called him Lunar. She just liked the name, saying it over and over to herself. Once she was back at school Lunar would take himself down to Annie's, returning to greet Grace from school. He would then stay with her all evening even going up to bed with her. Only when she was safely asleep would he pour himself out of her slightly open bedroom window into the night.

* * *

How fast the years fly past. Grace grew into an athletic, statuesque young woman, yet she was a quiet lass. She still loved the woods and plants, but knew it was time to make her own way in the world.

Grace had had to work so hard to get to university. She had no problem learning what to do for an injured animal, but was easily distracted from her school work. She would sit to do her homework only to find herself stroking Lunar or watching something in the garden or rain on the window or... When she had decided on a course in physiotherapy she made Leeds Beckett her first choice as she didn't want to be far away from home. A talented athlete, she had had to choose between training and revision. If only she had stuck to the javelin she might have made the junior England squad, but she had gone instead for the 100 metres. Not quite good enough! Yes, she dreamed of being an Olympian, winning even, but being a county athlete was not going to make a career. A sports physiotherapist then. Now in her third term she was really getting into the course and starting to make new friends. It had taken a while, perhaps because she had chosen to live out, a terraced house in Headingley shared with four others. But probably more that she was so very shy. In any case, it was the only way she could have Lunar with her and she would not go without him. He had grown into a chunky, handsome cat with a snow-white coat and deep green eyes. Whenever she caught the bus back to Cheryl and Annie, Lunar went with, cosily carried in a sports bag.

Here and now Grace was busy with her javelin training. Once she had exams out of the way she was looking forward to a summer competing. Grace smoothed her purple and black vest, she stood with her back to the stands, getting into her zone, breathing deep and slow, visualising the throw she was about to make. At 5' 11", well- muscled from gym work, her thick dark hair loosely bunched and flowing down her back she looked magnificent, a virago. Of course there was the scarring on her lip; she was not pretty, but she had a sculptural beauty and, yes, grace. She picked up her javelin, balancing it. Went through the throw again. Ready now, she walked to her mark. Wait. Balance. Go. "Haaar!" she shouted as she flung her spear. The javelin landed well up the field and she walked after it: pick it up, throw again. It was a good start, very pleasing. She went through the throw again in her mind, her arm automatically throwing an imaginary javelin. As Grace walked back to the covered rest area, she was looking for her coach. Instead, her eye caught a youth walking towards her. Not just any youth either: she had seen him with the sprint group in training, perfecting their starts, increasing leg speed. He was drop-dead gorgeous. Glance again: yes, definitely coming towards her.

"Hey, I've been watching you throw and I think you're amazing. Would you like to meet after this? Have a coffee?"

Grace looked at him very directly, her eyes searching his. Was he serious? Not doing this for a bet? He seemed taken aback, like he'd expected her to be all coy.

"You know Tiki's?" Grace asked, "Meet you there at five?"

Grace sounded cool, detached, but her heart was racing. She couldn't believe this beautiful boy was interested in her.

"Mint. See you then. I'm Thomas, by the way."

Well, that was the end of Grace's training session! Yep, focus right out the window! She spent the rest of the afternoon thinking about Thomas: not Tom, Thomas.

Thomas couldn't have been more charming. He paid for coffee and buns and seemed genuinely interested in Grace's plans for the future. He told her he was in his first year of medicine and that his dad had bought him a terraced house, where he chose to live alone, by way of investment. After the coffee Grace was smitten. Thomas was handsome, clever and rich. He gave her a lift home in his car. A car! Mum and her always went by bus.

As she opened the door of her scruffy Headingley home Lunar ran up as usual. "This yours?" said Thomas, reaching down to the cat. But instead of allowing himself to be stroked, Lunar pushed back on his haunches, mouth open and snarling, hissing with ears laid back. Quick as a flash he raked his claws along Thomas's outstretched hand. Grace didn't know what to say. She'd never seen Lunar like that before.

"It's nothing," said Thomas, reaching into his pocket for a tissue to wipe off the blood. "Hey, I'd like to see you again. I mean, it's tricky with exams and that, but how about a drink sometime?"

Wow! Of course she would love a drink with Thomas! They arranged to meet at the Skyrack on Wednesday.

Grace opened a tin of baked beans for her tea. Thomas Symcox, she said to herself, over and over, what a lovely name. Wednesday couldn't come soon enough.

Thomas was just as chuffed to have a date with Grace, although not for the same reasons. He had watched her train before and thought what a magnificent specimen she was. It was a pity about the lip and the lisp but he decided for his purposes it didn't matter, in fact he might investigate the lip and the jaw beneath. Before he killed her of course. Even better, she was a loner: her introversion and natural avoidance of others meant no Facebook or Twitter, no constant tagging or texting anyone else. He would have her to himself. In a couple of weeks' time a group of students from his year – he wouldn't call them friends exactly, well not at all, but he was sure he could get invited – were going to the coast for the weekend to celebrate the end of exams. He would take Grace with him. Yes, a day on the beach then as the others went off to the arcades he would whisk Grace away in Dad's little yacht. It was easy to handle alone. Out at sea he would have a heart to heart with Grace, so to speak. It was a pity he would have to drug her, but she was a big strong girl. He had the Rohypnol already. After he would dump her body, tied to gym weights, overboard, sail to another location and then, oh dear, the yacht would catch fire and sink and he would manage to swim ashore.

He took himself into his bedroom and pulled the silver toolbox from under the bed. Lovingly he went through his collection of surgical instruments: best of all, the sternal saw and chest clamps. Just handling them gave him a hard-on. Opening the wardrobe door where there was a long mirror, he dropped his trousers and wrapped his right hand around his erect cock. He stroked his torso, the rippling abdominal muscles, with the clamp. Imagine Grace bleeding and writhing beneath him, her heart pounding as if she were in a race, her blood flooding out and pooling as she died! It was a magnificent wank and the spunk shot out. Nearly into the toolbox, in fact – close shave! Thomas smiled to himself: the next time he knocked one out it would be over

Grace's exposed heart. Yes, he would save himself for Grace now. Anyway, he wanted to keep the girl keen for the next couple of weeks, the pub on Wednesday and maybe his sister's birthday dinner on Friday. Thank goodness he had the (genuine) excuse of exams not to see her too often, he might get away without even kissing her!

Wednesday went okay, he thought. She was wearing jeans and a vest top. You couldn't miss the bulging biceps, the powerful shoulders, even with the rich curtain of hair. Anyway, with the excuse of revision he was able to ditch her fast enough having delivered the invite to his sister's birthday dinner. She invited him in but he made a show of 'managing to resist' – what a gentleman!

Grace was both excited and nervous about Friday. Meeting his folks! Already! Would they like her? What should she wear?

At last Friday came and Grace had on her best top: sequins in black red and gold depicting a flame, the shape asymmetric with a broad strap over one shoulder, leaving the other bare. Then she had black jeans and flat black pumps. She wore her thick hair loose and no makeup. She hated when she felt taller than everyone else, and if she applied makeup it always looked as if it had been put on with a catapult. Thomas picked her up and said she looked lovely. His face didn't appear to agree with this statement, but still. He was just in jeans and a tee with a bright orange hoodie over it.

Off they went in his car, rather fast, to his parents' spread just south of Leeds. To Grace the house looked huge, bigger than High Moor. Thomas strode in through the front door, saw he had lost her on the driveway, walked back and towed her indoors. Jo and Geoff were both in the kitchen when they walked in, both in casual wear. They looked surprised to see Grace, probably because they were. At no point had they expected a 'plus one' from Thomas. He'd never even mentioned having a girlfriend. Anyway, Jo had made quite clear this was a family dinner. Ellie walked in and it was she who came to the rescue.

"Hey! You must be Thomas' new girlfriend, how lovely to meet you. When did you two get together?"

And she took Grace off into the garden, making her feel welcome, looking genuinely pleased with the small box of chocolates Grace had bought her. After all, Thomas had never bought her anything in his life.

Ellie thought this typical of her brother, to bring uninvited guests. And the poor girl was clearly out of her depth. And those clothes! She looked like she was going to a school disco!

Once Auntie Loo, Uncle Dave and various cousins had arrived, dinner was served and ALL had a good time. Grace sat quiet throughout, enjoying the food, listening attentively to the conversation. At the suggestion of charades after pudding Thomas took himself into the kitchen where he could quaff beer in peace, only to find he was followed by Grace, hopeful of some time alone together. Maybe Thomas would touch her, kiss her even. Thomas pasted on a smile and fetched her a beer. The kitchen window was wide open allowing the cool evening air to circulate and Grace felt chilly after the crowded dining room. She rubbed her arms to warm them up.

"Here, have this." Thomas pulled off his hoodie and stuffed it at Grace. Grace pulled it on, enjoying its soft warmth and the fact that she had something of HIS. It fitted exactly.

"Hey, Grace," Thomas looked like he had just had a eureka moment, "a load of my mates are off to the coast next weekend. Bum around on the beach, fish and chips, then hit the town for the night. We've a mini bus booked. I'd love it if you could come."

Well, what was to stop her? She was independent, grown-up Grace. "Wow, where on the coast? I love swimming in the sea! What time and where?" Not to seem too keen or anything.

"I'll get all the details and pop and see you, like, Wednesday?"

Grace couldn't wait.

It was Jo who ordered a taxi to take Grace home since Thomas seemed to have overdone the beer. The time had flown and now it was near midnight, Thomas had spread himself over a couch in the hall and couldn't be arsed to get up for Grace, so Ellie walked with her to the waiting taxi. Ellie thought Grace a sweet girl, too sweet and innocent for her brother. He had never bought any girls home but had been seen on occasion with flash pretty things and never the same one twice, but here was Grace, striking yes, those strong limbs, but very plain. She didn't know how to say what she wanted to say.

"Grace," she started, looking into the happy eyes of the young woman as she turned towards her. "Grace, be careful, you will, won't you? Don't let him hurt you."

Grace took this as meaning: 'Don't let him break your heart because he's rich and you're a pauper'. She covered the slim hand of Ellie's that earnestly gripped her arm with her own broad hand and gave a squeeze, a smile, a nod. With that she got into the taxi paid for by Geoff Symcox and went home at a more sedate speed than the one she'd arrived at.

Grace woke late the next morning, she was dreaming of being suffocated, horrid! Half asleep her hands went to her face. Good lord, Lunar was practically sat on her head!

"Silly boy!" she laughed. "I thought I was dying! S'pose you're ready to go home, eh?" She rubbed the head and ears of the beautiful cat and he threw himself against her, as if he couldn't get close enough. She got up and dressed hurriedly, throwing on the orange hoodie, now a piece of toast, a swig of milk... Within the hour Lunar was peeping out of the sports bag as they rode the bus out of Leeds to see Cheryl and Annie Haggie.

You could get off the bus not very far from where Matty had been dumped by Jo several years ago and walk through the wood, if you knew the deer paths, closely covered as they were, right to Deepwood itself. Grace went this way now, feeling tired by her late night, enjoying the relative cool of the wood, away from the shimmering heat out in the sunshine. June was turning out to be a scorcher. She threaded her way between the trunks of horse chestnut and sycamore and pushed through elderberry and hawthorn in the clearings. As they neared the edge of the wood, Lunar dropped himself out of the bag: he knew his way from here and would rock up at the cottages, well, when he felt like it.

Reaching Deepwood, Grace creaked open the gate and walked through the echinacea, rudbeckia and geranium that overlay the path, the cottage itself nestling in verdant summer growth, the door partially obscured by buddleia and a fuchsia bush that had evaded pruning. A hen sunbathed on the doorstep. Grace walked in to find Annie busy stirring a herby soup in a copper pan over the fire. Annie waved for Grace to sit down; she'd have a brew going in a tick. Grace dumped herself down on the settee and reluctantly dragged off the orange hoodie – it was absolutely roasting in here! She picked Frisbee off the arm of the settee and kissed him firmly before setting him on her lap. She yawned widely. Annie regarded her closely. She knew about the young man.

She knew he was bad news, the cards had told her, but how to broach it to Grace? Look at her face! All dreamy and loved up! This gentle girl who wore her heart on her sleeve...

Then they both heard an engine, Ike driving down the lane to see Annie. Before long there was the sound of Matty's excited barking as he bounded down the path ahead of Ike. That dog! Still full of beans, still bouncing all over everyone! He had grown into a fine dog. May had his hair trimmed so you never noticed the lack of pinnas. There was a fluffy tuft on the stump of his tail. Annie braced herself to get bounced on, but Matty ran three strides into the room and stopped as if he'd been shot, nearly flipping himself over. He raised his head. Sniff, sniff! And then he turned unbelievably fierce, his eyes slits, his lips rolled back over his teeth. Unrecognisable, honestly. Then he launched himself at the hoodie on the settee beside Grace, tearing into it where it lay.

Ike had caught up with Matty now. "Hey! Drop that! Let go!" commanded Ike, catching hold of Matty's collar whilst pulling at the hoodie. "What's up w'ya?" He pulled Matty back by his collar and the dog continued to whine and growl.

"Is that his?" Annie asked Grace.

"His?" For a second Grace looked confused. "Oh, yes, yes, it's Thomas's. Was. Why would Matty do that?" Grace took the torn top from Ike, held it up, seeing how bad the tears were, seeing if she could mend it.

"He remembers, you see," Annie said, eyes bright, urgent. She was out of her chair by the fire and up to Grace, trying to deflect her attention from the hoodie. "Grace, Thomas, he hurt Matty, do y'see? The cards said so."

Grace looked aghast at Annie. Was she for real? Exasperated she turned to Ike; would he set Annie straight?

"He niver forgets a scent, lass," said Ike. His faith in Annie was absolute: history had proved all her predictions correct.

"I meet a gorgeous, rich bloke and you want me to give him up because a dog bites a shirt?" Were these clowns jealous or something?

"But the cards..." insisted Annie. "I didn't know how to tell you..."

"Yeh, the cards." Grace rolled her eyes.

"What about Lunar? Does he like this Thomas?"

Grace would have liked to say yes, but, let's face it, the cat hated him. She picked Frisbee back off the floor where he seemed to have fallen, lifting him so his fluffy nose met hers, "You too, I s'pose!" The flash of red from his eyes was so bright, Grace almost got whiplash. She shot her head back so fast, her eyes losing focus for a second.

"Listen to the animals, Grace!" Annie, bending above her, her hand an iron grip on Grace's.

"Don't squash Frisbee," Grace said quietly, stroking the plush fur and feeling like she was going to cry. *Please don't let me cry*, she thought.

"At least don't go to the coast at the weekend," pleaded Annie.

"Coast?" *So the cards had told Annie that too*, thought Grace. "I'll think about it. I really will." said Grace. And she meant it.

That evening Grace was laid on her bed, the window open wide though the bedroom was cooler than outside. Lunar sat on the window sill, studying the garden, long tail hanging into the room, its end flicking now and then. Cheryl had accosted her when she got home, wanting to know what was wrong. Then she had cried. She couldn't help herself. Then she blubbed the whole story out about Matty and that. Mum had wanted to know why she had never been round to Thomas's if it was his house. "Probably got a torture chamber in the cellar, love. He's one o' them weirdos, get rid." Well, easy for her to say, isn't it?

Sighing, Grace picked up her phone. What is it folks always said? 'If it seems too good to be true, it is.' And Thomas' sister, the warning, what had she meant? After starting, deleting, starting, deleting, Grace finally texted, "It was good to meet your family last night but it made me realise how different we are. I don't think we should meet any more but hope we can be friends. See you on the track sometime." Press send. Then she blocked his phone. Was it mean to text? She didn't think she could hold her reserve if they met. She could hear Cheryl in the kitchen, clearing up dinner pots. She lay back, squeezing the last tears she would cry for Thomas Symcox from her eyes and drifted to sleep. Lunar looked round at her, then dropped silently into the garden.

Thomas had the television on without really watching it, his thoughts on details for the coast trip, when the text came through. He sat up quick, sharp. "Stupid cow!" He texted back some slobbery, heartbroken message, then realised she'd blocked him. He shoved the phone in his pocket and grabbed the car keys: he would have to talk her round. Like he needed this! He was straight round to her terrace, he wouldn't have given a stuff about the time anyhow, but it wasn't late. Banged on the door. It seemed an age before it was opened by a skinny girl with pink hair and multiple earrings but some swotty secretary specs on.

"Grace in?" Thomas, abrupt, trying hard to hold his temper.

"She goes home for the weekend," says Skinny.

"Where's home? I need to speak with her."

Skinny leaves the door open and Thomas follows her in, turns out she's looking for an address.

"It's here somewhere," she says. "Ah, there you go." She shoves an envelope at Thomas. A man calls from upstairs and Skinny gesticulates for him to leave.

Thomas put the postcode on the envelope into the satnav and followed the instructions out to Highmoor farm. It only took him 25 minutes, speeding where he could. Even as he hit the rough chalk track to the farm, he was still doing 50. The satnav told him to take a right up to the farm, but he saw the cottages straight ahead, he accelerated forward. Here a drainage channel had been cut to prevent rainwater running down the hill and eroding the track. It required steady negotiation with a car, so, speeding, Thomas bounced down it, snagging the bumper on the far side of the channel. The car jolted to a halt and stalled. Thomas pulled himself out and surveyed the front of the car for damage. Only the bloody bumper. He pulled it free. Looking on, he could see the track didn't improve from here: not far to go, he decided, so he left the car where it was and walked.

Which cottage did she live in? He checked the envelope in his pocket then hammered on the ancient oak door with his fist, only then noticing the knocker, a wrought iron ring held in a lion's mouth. It seemed an age before he heard movement behind the door, then at last it was opened by a heavy woman with thick hair falling over her shoulders, coarse-featured and heavy-browed. She was sweating slightly and Thomas was aware of the smell of her body overlaid by the scent of cheap perfume. Like her daughter, she looked strong and capable.

"Would it be possible for me to speak to Grace, please?" Thomas managed polite.

Cheryl took in the young man in front of her, the immaculate hair, designer clothes. So this was the dog abuser.

"No," she said and slammed the door in his face. He heard a heavy bolt draw shut behind the door.

"Grace," he shouted to the upstairs windows, "Grace, I love you, can we talk? Please?"

The sound of the window above the door opening. Thomas looked up and got a jug of urine full in the face. The window shut.

"Fuck!" Thomas tried to shake the wet away. "Bitches!" He would have to try to get to Grace through the week. Angrily he stomped back the car. Then as he passed the gate post at the end of the drive to the cottages there was that cat, the white thing, sitting on the post looking smug. He swiped out at it and surprised both himself and the cat by catching it by the tail. Thomas grinned, "Aw, poor pussy, you're for it now!" Lunar struggled and writhed, but the grip on his tail was iron. Finally he dangled in Thomas's hand, held well away from his body. Thomas then swung him up and banged him down on the ground and whilst Lunar was dazed and before the cat could gain any purchase on the chalk road, Thomas placed his booted foot across his neck. Then Thomas pressed down, crushing the cat's trachea. Lunar clawed frantically, but his claws made no impression on the quality leather boot, and anyway he was still so stretched out while his tail was so hard held. Thomas watched the chest heave as it tried to draw in air, heard the strangled gasps for oxygen, watched the slowing paddling, fighting limbs. He released the pressure on the cat's neck, no fun in it dying too quick. A greedy gasp for life, respite, then the boot was down once more.

"Bye, bye now," smirked Thomas as he pressed the life from the animal, watching the tongue swell, the eyes pop. When Lunar was dead, the once bright green eyes clouding already, Thomas once again held him aloft by the tail inspecting his handiwork before tossing Lunar into the ditch collecting the runoff from the drainage channel. Could he ever be found in that watery grave?

At exactly that moment Haggie Annie, crocheting coasters for selling door to door, ceased in her labours. Was that a cat wailing she heard? A single cry of pain? She dropped a stitch. Instinct would lead her to recover the body of the cat within the hour of his killer putting the broken bumper of his car across the back seat and speeding back up the track as fast as he'd come down it. Annie set about digging the cat a proper grave in her garden. The ground was rock hard and it was dark by the time she was done.

Now Haggie Annie sat hands on knees on a stool in front of her fire. She knew that Grace was still in danger. She looked across at Frisbee perched on the back of the settee.

"Well, I'm game if you are," she said. The glass eyes gleamed. She pulled herself off the stool by holding the mantelpiece and reached up to a small wooden chest in a cove above the fire. It contained special ingredients: toad poison, bat blood, her crystals. Along with hair from Lunar's tail and a piece of the orange hoodie, she wove a powerful spell. As her mutterings reached their climax, a sudden wind blew around Deepwood, banging the shutters, swirling dust. The chickens awoke on their perches. "Oooaar!" they said.

Thomas called round at Grace's Headingley home on Monday evening. This time the door was opened by a short stocky girl, the sides of her head shaved beneath a mop of black hair.

"What?" she said, before Thomas had a chance to speak. Her posture aggressive she blocked the door with her solid little body. Exasperated, Thomas realised he was going to have to rethink his plans for Grace. He had swung his invite to the beach at the weekend by befriending a pretty little thing, Sandhya, on his course. Well, actually she came and spoke to him. Yeh, do you know, Sandhya might do for the boat trip, I mean, she said she couldn't swim. Bet Grace could swim like a dolphin, hard to say she had drowned! Oh, he would do Grace one day, she deserved it now; he would just have to think of a new plan for her. And perhaps it would be useful to practise on someone, hone his technique for Grace?

Saturday dawned clear and bright. Even at 10 in the morning it was hot, promising a scorching day. Some of the beach-goers nursed banging heads after a Friday celebration of the end of exams. Not Thomas, though, he kept a clear head, confident he had done well in the written papers. He was excited about today, though – absolutely buzzing! His Friday evening had been spent preparing the yacht. Tools, ties, petrol. A bottle of champagne. He might not even use the Rohypnol, she was only little. He picked up Sandhya and her friend Mags. Christ, how much gear did they need? They looked like they were going for a week!

"We've got to get changed for the club later," says Mags. "And we've got the cricket stuff."

They jammed everything in Thomas' motor and soon caught up with the minibus with everyone else in. Thomas followed it out to Fraisthorpe. Both in the back seat, they giggled over videos from the night before and chatted about the holiday ahead. Did they never shut up? Thomas thought about his duct tape and how much he'd like to slap it over Sandhya's mouth, like now!

Sandhya had only spoken to Thomas as she perceived him as a lonely outsider; she was just being kind. Now she felt he had latched on to her like a sticky bob to a sock: I mean, what was all this about a sail out in some yacht? She had made sure she had Mags with her in the car and she would work out a way to swerve the boat trip later. Her instincts told her to be careful, though, because Thomas was a little too pushy, a little bit weird. She made sure she stuck with everyone else as they left the car park and carried their gear onto the beach. The tide was well out, in fact on the turn, but they had plenty of time for sunbathing. There were families and couples there already so they wandered off down the beach to find a space suitable for their cricket match. Mags stripped down to a tiny bikini and slapped on sun cream. Sandhya tied her long black hair up and kicked off her shoes: her pedal pushers and tee were staying on!

Beers were cracked open but even as everyone was getting settled, Miles, the bossy organiser, was pressing the stumps into the sand.

"C'mon!" he shouted. "We need two teams..."

Mags rolled her eyes, "May as well get it over with." The girls ran, walked or dragged themselves, depending on the individual level of enthusiasm, to join the game, Miles already sorting people into teams. A coin was tossed, putting the 'Jellyfish' squad into bat. Sandhya was first to bat and she waved it in front of her like a tennis racket. She caught the foam ball on the edge of the bat and it flew high in the air prescribing a sharp parabola and heading fast to Thomas on long stop. "Catch!" yelled his team mates. The ball twonked him on the head and bounced off into the sand. Universal groan. Well, Thomas's attention was somewhere else: he was watching an old lady who had placed her folding chair a little down the beach from them. Thomas waved to the others, pointing to the old dear and they reluctantly interrupted their game to see what had caught his attention.

Well, this old love, wearing a cotton dress and a much darned cardigan, short Wellingtons on her feet, a headsquare over her long grey hair, had a soft toy dog in one hand, a squeaky ball in the other. The toy dog had on a red collar to match the lead from which it had been unclipped, this still tied to the leg of the chair. She threw the ball. "Fetch it! Good boy!" she said to the toy dog before throwing it after the ball. Then she strode across the sand and picked both up. "Good boy, good dog," she said.

They watched a couple of throws, then Miles reinstated the game. I mean, whatever makes you happy. The dotty old lady did no harm. Only Thomas continued to watch. The next ball landed fairly near so he picked it up.

He thought he might lob it into the sea but in the end he allowed the woman to walk up to him. She held out her hand for the ball, the dog cuddled close. Thomas handed it to her and as he did their fingers touched. Despite the heat of the day a shiver went down his spine, the hairs standing up on the back of his neck. He looked into her eyes, bright eyes, too young for the face. "Thank you, dear," she said. Scowling, he turned back to the game.

The girls soon became bored with cricket and the game dissolved into mayhem; no one was sure who won. They spread themselves on their towels, pushing back hair, swigging lukewarm water from plastic bottles. An ice cream van arrived in the car park. People started to make their way up the beach for ice cream, soon joined by a contingent from our medical students. "Get us a 99, please!" from one, "Any orange flavoured lolly!" from another.

Thomas sat cross-legged on the sand near the girls, he couldn't be bothered to go all the way over to the car park. Then he noticed the old lady clip her toy dog back to the chair leg. With the instruction to "Sit, Stay!" she followed the lads up the beach. "She'll be gone ages," thought Thomas. Time to have some fun at the mad old bag's expense. Her touch had unnerved him, he wanted to get his own back.

Watched lazily by Sandhya and Mags he strode over to the dog, placed on its own towel, shaded by the chair. Unclipping it, he lifted it to take a closer look and it grabbed him. No, seriously: it was like a powerful magnetic pull and in the next second it had its jaws round his windpipe. He gasped for breath, pulling at the toy, but it felt like iron, its grip vice-like. He raised a hand, waved at the girls. It did look funny, it looked as if he held the toy to his neck, pretending attack. Mags cheered and waved. Very good! And now here were the ice creams: the girls turned their attention to licking dribbles from cones, pulling Fabs out of wrappers.

But the iron grip stayed on Thomas' neck: he fell to his knees, his vision blurring, flashes behind his eyes. His hands had let go of the dog and he now pawed ineffectively at the sand. As his chest heaved and his heart pounded his last thought was of the white cat in the chalk dust of the track.

No one noticed the old lady returning. She picked up the dog and put him carefully in her patchwork bag, folded up her chair and, leaving Thomas face down on the towel, shuffled up the beach. Soon a broad man walking with a russet dog, bouncing around despite the heat and the long walk through the dunes, caught her up and relieved her of the chair. Back at the car park they scrambled aboard his flat deck and drove off back towards Leeds.

Sandhya did see Thomas on the towel. Anti-social sod, sunbathing over there, she thought.

The tide seemed to race in and the students began packing their stuff ready to hit Brid. Sandhya ran her eye over the beach to see if Thomas was about but the tide was well up over where he had been lying.

"Lover boy must have left," teased Mags coming up behind Sandhya.

"Give over, he was creeping me out! C'mon, let's catch up with the others, get on that minibus." Wooping, they did a half run up the beach. *Good, no boat trip!* thought Sandhya.

The incoming tide had lifted Thomas up, strong undertows catching his corpse, dragging him down and away from land, all the way out to the North Sea. Here the boggle-eyed creatures of the deep would pick his bones clean.

TASTE THE RAIN

THE RAIN WAS driving into my face as the quad lurched along the narrow muddy track. I had been longer at the top field than expected, having to catch Basil, Pa's favourite ram, to remove a briar from between his cleats. Wouldn't be getting round the ewes if he were lame. Now I was caught out by the rapidly fading light and struggling to hold my course, hardly helped by the feeble lights on the quad. An exhilarating ride, bouncing along the muddy ruts of the track, my hood pulled back so I can see better. I can feel my fringe plastered to my head and the cold rain run down my face, filling my mouth as I gasp for breath. Such short days in December. I glimpse Seb's tail in the lights, running low and fast ahead and to the left of me. My faithful border collie, racing me back to the farm. Food and warmth. We bounce into a small yard lit by the warm glow of light from the kitchen window at one side and the strip lights on in the cow shed ahead. I drive the quad into one of the stables, kill the engine. My fingers are frozen despite protective mitts on the handlebars, so I struggle with the padlock and hasp to lock the bike away. Seb is already in the dog stable, top door always shut, lower door always open, so the dogs can go in and out as they please. The dogs always gave visitors a lively welcome. In a hurry to get done, I go for the dog's tea in the feed shed in the dark, tripping over discarded bags and string, cursing to myself. I'm determined not to turn the light on now! Scoop a load of dry food into each of the four bowls and round to the dogs: Seb and Bob, the collies, Jimmy and Rex, the terriers. The bowls are set down while the dogs sit, waiting for my permission to move. Good boys, 'Eat!' and up they jump and gollop the food down.

As I make my way to the cowshed to see what Pa is up to, one of the ponies neighs to me. Pa must be busy with the heifer if he hasn't got round to haying the horses yet. They get a good pile of our sweet meadow hay. Summer in a bale. "Good girls," I say as I rub fuzzy foreheads under thick forelocks. If I'm honest, I'm dragging my feet a little. Pa's been waiting for this heifer to calve, caught by the bull too early. Ideally she would calve in the spring when she had a little bit more frame. I didn't fancy a difficult birth just now. After dinner perhaps. But there she is, licking a fine bull calf. Good news. But there, washing the birth fluids from his bare upper torso with what must be freezing water, is Daaave. Bad news. It's 'Dave', really, but he speaks right slow, if he speaks at all, so he calls his self Daaave.

It's a delight to watch the heifer, the calf already making an effort to stand. And it takes my eyes away from Dave and the terrible burns that run across most of his body. It's been said he was in a house fire a few years back; a miracle he escaped alive. "Hey, Dave, good job, he looks a belter. Where's me Pa?" I enquire.

Dave always avoids eye contact and he mumbled his reply into the thick sweater he was now putting on. "Yer mam called cos yer Pa's taken badly."

Pa reckoned he was sickening for something this morning, poor Pa. "Are you coming in fer yer tea?" I ask, be rude not to.

Dave nods his reply and, with a last check of mother and baby, we make our way to the fuggy warmth of Mum's kitchen. I know it's not his fault, but Dave's burns go up his neck, round his mouth... and his ear is gone... Anyway, he eats worse than Seb. Sometimes I don't know where to look, with the result I always try to sit next to him. Out of the line of sight. Even then he has a strange smell about him. Fusty, like he's been shut in a drawer and forgotten.

Mum has a mutton pie fresh out the oven, with leeks from her vegetable plot and a thick gravy. I feel a bit guilty, sitting down to this when Pa is in bed with orange juice. He has flu. Proper flu, where you're freezing one minute and dripping sweat the next. "Well, he wouldn't go for a jab, would he? Like I told him. Picked it up from the market I'll bet..." nagged on Mum, "...so I called Dave and here he was just in time, pulled the calf without the need of the jack..."

You have to admit Dave is dead useful. Not the biggest of men and yet he's as strong as a bull. There's endless tales of Dave's strength. Lifting trailers, pulling horses out of bogs. All sorts. He works for anyone, a phone call away. Probably pleased to leave the shack he calls home. Water from a spring and no electric. Ha, like here in a bad storm! "

Well, anyway," continues Mum, "it means you'll have to go to the wedding. We've got Dave."

Omigod, no way, not me, hate useful Dave, I'd have to leave tomorrow. My laden fork is poised between my plate and my mouth. "Can't Dave do the wedding?" I hear myself say. Mum bangs the gravy ladle down with more force than is necessary.

It's my cousin's wedding and Mum and Pa were due to go the next day with me happily on farm duty. I know she was dying to go. London and everything. She had been to York for a hat. Even with Pa poorly I never in a million years thought she would miss it. I went to London once, on a school trip. There, I've been! No need to go again. I've nowt to wear. Well, dealer boots and jeans obviously, but no girlie stuff, no posh hat. Still, I see someone should represent our family and my daddy needs looking after. So I'll go.

Later Mum and I go through my wardrobe in search of a suitable outfit and we find a trouser suit bought when I was at college. Hey, no one will be looking at me. Mum starts fiddling with my hair, she's attacking me with a hairbrush. "Look at these split ends!" she says. "It needs a trim. You're so pretty," she says, "why do you have to be such a tomboy?"

I can see my reflection in the mirror on the back of the wardrobe door. The face looking at me has blue eyes and a pert, freckled nose. The mouth is full, with permanent creases at the side, like you would draw a smiley cartoon mouth. My hair is long, because I can't be bothered to get it cut, and auburn. Pa says I look okay. Anyway, there's no way Mum is getting near my hair with a pair of scissors! I wrestle Mum for the hairbrush and we fall back on the bed, laughing.

"I'm sorry you're not going," I say.

"Can't be helped. Do you want to borrow the hat?" she replies.

"THE hat! For a December wedding!" As if. "I'm taking me beanie!" I laugh. Together we pack me a small case.

Dave doesn't go home, he takes the rather damp spare bedroom complete with single bed and sagging mattress. I tell you, however he slept it was better than what I did. I was bricking it. Toss, turn, toss. I worried about the bus, missing the train, finding my way across London. Despite our differences, I get on well with my cousin, Steve, but I have nothing to say to his fiancée, Julia. I just don't get needing your eyebrows shaping, having false claws – sorry, nails – glued on. What a waste of money! And she must think me a right dung ball. So I'm sure she's a nice person. But.

Mum was a city girl, her family coming up to Yorkshire for holidays. She met Pa and the rest is history. Cousin Steve is her sister's son, always lived and worked in London. Can't imagine him with dirt under his nails. I haven't seen him since I was 10.

Eventually I fell to sleep five minutes before the alarm went off. Well, it feels like that, doesn't it?

It seemed another five minutes before Mum is force-feeding me toast, still trying to tidy my mop of hair, fussing. We'll be late for the bus if I don't get a move on. Aw, shame! Glancing across the yard Dave is starting up the quad ready to do the sheep rounds. Seb dances round him all excited. Traitor! There's the first streak of light on the horizon, it's cold. Cold and damp.

There were a few people on board the Coastliner bus when the rest of us board at Malton. It's the first bus of the day and not quite light. I zip upstairs and grab the seat right at the front next to the window, my bag on the shelf in front. Then this big bloke comes up and sits next to me, despite there being more than half a bus empty, his meaty thigh pressing against mine. Man sitting. As if! As we leave for York I concentrated on looking out the window, legs turned away from Fatty. It was starting to snow, big wet slushy flakes. We're zipping along, the fug over the bus windows partially obscuring the view. Now on single carriageway, woodland on either side, when a deer leaps out in front of the car in front of the bus. The car hits the deer. The bus spins wildly on the slush, aquaplaning across the road. People are screaming and the big bloke too close to my side is thrown toward me, pinning me to the damp window, my cheek pressed to the cold damp glass. The bus is going over! Over on its side, blocking the lane for oncoming traffic. I know I am going to die. So sorry, Ste, not to make the wedding. My heart is pounding with fear, I'm struggling to achieve a position away from the window but we are flung downwards fast. There's a flash, in my head I think, then darkness and silence. There's no pain, though I feel a pulling sensation from my spine up through my body. It was strange, seeing this little white ghost trying to leave my body. Other ghosties were drifting up from people's bodies then dissipating into the air, but I was under the fat man, soaked in blood from the gash in his neck. My body re- absorbed the ghost and soon I could hear the heavy clank of chains. Some lumbering creature hooked a chain onto fat man and I am dragged away too. Glued with his blood. I see my body left behind, the broken skull and mangled right arm. The fat man sees me stuck to him and manages to leer at me even though we're dead.

Down and down we go. I can't feel much, but the air becomes increasingly stale. I must have passed out although it felt more like falling asleep. When I wake I am in a pile of, of what? People? Souls? I am dragged out and plomped onto my feet by a huge ugly beastly biped. There are several of them around us. In my head I came to think of them as the grunts. Along with the others in my pile we are being sorted out and after a bit of prodding and poking two of the grunts have a bit of a scrap over me. Never felt so wanted. Finally I am herded into a small group and we are pushed down a long corridor to our place of work. Although there aren't any lights I can see adequately. My vision is different somehow. Feeling my face I find I only have one eye and that pretty central in my face, a small flat nose beneath and a slit of a mouth. My skin feels rough, scaly even. Yes, I see now, I *am* scaly. I have always been right-handed but now my right arm is altogether shorter than my left. It has three claws and the left hand has five. My head has some spiny protrusions.

I have a little tail. I like the legs, though: well-muscled with useful clawed feet. So pretty... Not. No one has clothes. Everyone is grey. Actually, everything is grey. Some souls are soft and squashy, some fuzzy. When I try to talk to the others I can manage a grunt. No voice. We can hiss, like a threatened cat, or grunt. Apart from the shuffle of feet, then, our progress is silent.

Ahead there is a larger space, brighter with the glare of molten lava and very hot. Lava is gushing and spinning like whirlpools in a river and within I can see faces, screaming, limbs on fire reaching out. A sharp prod from behind. A shovel is pushed into my hand and I am directed towards an empty flume. I see now: we are shoring up a wall to redirect the lava flow. Then we have rocks to move. Then lava to stir, the hands of the burning snatching at our shovels. One soul is pulled in... Scream. Grunt, hiss and scream. After what felt like forever, my muscles aching, so tired, we are herded up a short passage to a feeding area. Grey slop is poured into large communal bowls and it's everyone for themselves, snarling and hissing and pushing for food. I'm not much of a fighter, but I'm in with the rest of them, desperate for a share. I had been starving before the meal; now I just felt hungry. And thirsty. At last it's rest time. How I'd love a long soak in the bath. No bath here. No bathroom. Food in one hole and out the other end, wherever you happened to be apparently. But really, in the sleeping area? We all found ourselves a space with much grunting and hissing if you touched anyone else. At first it was deliciously cool, but I soon felt cold. Since the sleeping area doubled up as a latrine we were laid in stinking mud, holding and glutinous. Curling into a foetal position, head on my forearms, I welcome sleep. And I barely seem to have slept at all when we are being whipped up back to work.

* * *

How long have I been here? Sometime between a long time and forever. I know how to make the food, have cleaned the sleeping area, have built the walls that control the lava flow. New souls arrive all the time and old ones fall into the lava or fall and are trodden into the mud floors, their eyes staring up at you as you walk over them. Hey, they improve the grip, right? If ever any sort of a bond is made with another we are separated, so I am used to being alone. And I work, my muscles hard as steel. Only in my dreams is there any escape. Last night I dreamt I was back on the moor, a skylark singing high above. Then, borne on the softest breeze on this summer day, a shower of rain. The petrichor fills my nostrils and big fresh drops of moisture track down my face. The dream is so real I can taste the rain. Back to reality: a murmur is travelling across the chamber, through the tunnels, the chief grunt doing his rounds. Perhaps it is the Devil himself! We fall to our knees, hoping not to get picked out. When he stops at a soul he commands, "Look at me…" and they do, then scream as their eyes are burned from their heads. Then we are back to our work, the victims of Chief Grunt struggling to work sightless, whipped for not keeping up, falling into the lava to burn forever.

Suddenly there's a commotion near the food hall. Grunts are leaving us – unheard of – and running up the slopes, up the ladders from the deeper passages and they are fighting. We can hear the growls, the clash of steel on steel, but just stand like so many sheep, waiting to see what happens next. Should I try to escape? Which way is out? Then the enemy are on us. To me they just look like our own grunts so when a bunch of us are herded up I think nothing of it. Could do with a change! We plod up to the feeding area and are whipped and shoved by our captors through a breach in the wall by the feed area. After a short, close passage we enter a huge cave. It isn't possible to see the outer walls, but I can feel the movement of air…and I can see the lava flow hundreds of feet below. We are now on a narrow path, the drop to my right and a vertical wall to my left. I've never been good with heights and I'm gluing myself to that wall. Then begins our journey down. Now and then segments of path break away, falling down to the burning river below, sometimes carrying a soul along too. I am relieved when we turn off this path into another tunnel. How airless it is. So humid. Our way now is lit by torches carried by the grunts and soon our progress stops. As we shuffle along and I see a hole in the tunnel floor, a vertical vent to the bubbling lava below. I am prodded in the back. We've to jump the hole. It's only four feet across, a long stride. My heart pounding, I give it my best jump and land on the soul that jumped before me. "Aagh! Sss!" it says, and I get a smack on the head. I feel myself falling back, then the grunt on the landing side grabs me by the arm and pulls me back. Having fought for me, it isn't going to let me go easily. Down still further we reach a honeycomb of tunnels dimly lit by torches; we weave our way to a cavern flooded with water, a little muddy beach strewn with slimy, smelly weed. We are lined up. There is the gentle lapping of waves on the shore, then, suddenly, like crocodiles out of a lagoon, creatures the size of a large bear surge onto the beach, their dripping skins glistening in the torchlight. There must be a dozen, all told, and they trail on short legs with webbed feet to the head of the line. Each soul is inspected – if they look strong they are hooked onto a rope, three or four to each, then dragged into the underground sea by one of the sea beasts. The few that are rejected are immediately set upon by grunts and eaten alive. Chief inspection creature reaches me. Wow, it is ugly: bulging eyes, a round head, tiny ears. It's interested in my scales, lifting one on my arm with a claw on its broad webbed hand. I pull back, hissing: it hurts! The creature has pincered the scale and pulls it off. Quickly it grabs my arm and inspects where the scale was. We nearly bump foreheads as I do the same. There, underneath, is pink skin, fresh and clean as around a healing wound. Seabeastie seems very perturbed by this. "Aaargh!" it shrieks, slapping its hands to its head, tromping round in circles. He calls over a grunt and I'm feeling more and more like I'm going to be dinner. Instead, the grunt, grumbling and moaning, herds me away from the water's edge. With his torch guiding the way we retrace our steps through the honeycomb of tunnels back to the one we arrived from. It shoves me towards the tunnel we arrived through and stomps away, the light diminishing as he goes. Soon I am in total darkness. I am supposed to return to the higher tunnels then. What else is there for me to do? I start up the tunnel, immediately stumbling and smacking my head on the wall. In the end I resort to crawling, don't want to plop down that vertical shaft.

As when driving in fog, distance seems to become extended. Surely I should have reached the shaft by now? Or have I gone the wrong way? And then my hand disappears into the void. So I've just got to jump the hole, right? My heart is hammering as I stand, feeling up the walls of the tunnel to keep myself straight, toes on the lip of the shaft. One, two, three, JUMP, as far as I can, landing on a firm surface. Sigh of relief, back to crawling. My knees are getting sore now so it's a relief to reach the cavern and stand. The lava below gives a red glow, the path like a dark ribbon along the cliff side ahead. It is easier to ascend the path than coming downhill earlier.

At last I stumble through the wall breach into the food hall. Three of the grunts are sat on the floor, happily engaged in eating somebody. Somebody furry. They stare at me. I stare at them. Then one lumbers over and picks me up by my head crest. And it falls off. It's left holding the crest as I feel up to my head find a rather sticky mat of hair. Not only that, but more of the scales have fallen off during my crawl along the tunnel. The grunts look at each other and after a shrug I am sent to the sleeping area. No food then.

Here I am again, busy building mud walls when the familiar wave of tension, the murmur of fear reaches us. We kneel. A grunt walks down the line and I am prodded on the shoulder. Boss grunt stands in front of me: "Look at me" he says. Slowly I raise my eyes to his and... he... is... beautiful! His golden skin like the shiniest racehorse ever, with muscle definition to match. He looks like a golden Anubis, with a lion tail. His eyes are tawny, warm. He looks up and down at himself, running his hands up and down his torso and along his arms. "Ha," he smiles, "when you look at me you see the mirror of your own soul. If I don't like what you see I burn out your eyes. But I like this. Yes, very good."

Lifting my arm, he studies the pink skin where so many scales have fallen away. "You are in the wrong place," he says, a look of concern on his face, "I will give you back to the living. Now, step into the light."

Suddenly I am surrounded by a bright light and I step into its warm glow. I taste honey, I'm going all relaxed... then I feel stabbing pain. I can barely breathe as my lungs fill with acrid smoke and I am pinned down by something heavy into a hard frame. With my free hand, the left, I reach to my face, where the pain is sharpest and, yes, I feel my eyeball resting on my shattered cheek. Bus! I'm back in the bus! Then I hear the chains. I have got to get out. I am covered in blood from the big man laying across me which makes things slippery, but, oh, I am so strong now. I reach up and grab the seat across the aisle and pull myself up with one arm. My legs are good so, choking and spluttering, I climb out of the broken window of the bus and slide down the roof to the ground. People are shouting. There are sirens. I stagger forward, past the car, the occupants safe already in an ambulance, past the deer, her soul long departed. And I Live.

* * *

How on Earth, or rather, how the Hell, did I survive? Especially considering where I was sitting in the bus. Everyone wanted to know. I'd been so lucky. I had lost my right eye and there was scarring to my face. The hair on that side was none too good either, but it would grow back. My right arm was badly damaged and it was now shorter, with the thumb and first two fingers remaining. Of course, my recovery has been meteoric: the consultants at the hospital cannot believe how quickly I have become used to one eye and a short arm. It's as if my arm was always deformed, so little surgery was required on it. They don't know that some of the work of the underworld has not been undone, or I could not have lived. Anyway, I've had forever to adjust to my disability, haven't I? There is talk of further surgery, cosmetic stuff, but I don't care how I look. I just want to be back on the farm.

* * *

Back home at last, never mind that it's raining. Again. Dave is here and we are preparing the barn for the March lambing mules. We are making large pens for holding expectant ewes, then passageways to lambing pens and a hospital area. Every year Pa and I have put some of the hurdles in at the wrong angle so later we are struggling to carry twins while the ewe follows and every year we forget what we had to do to fix the job! Dave is far more methodical, checking all the gates so the flow of sheep is favourable, the gates easy to manage. We work easily together, each knowing what the other wants. It only when Pa returns dripping from the fields we realise the time. We head in for lunch. Dave and I push each other to get through the half-closed barn door like a couple of kids. There is a niff of the stale odour from him so familiar to me now. I smell it on myself sometimes as I dress or even after a bath. Not the smell of the unclean but of the undead. I never said anything to anyone about the whole underworld thing. Instinct says not to.

As I cross the yard the skies really open, water bouncing off the roofs, jumping over the gutters. I tilt back my head and stick out my tongue, letting the raindrops run into my mouth. The taste of the rain is just as I dreamt it, the sweet taste of freedom. Wet clothes are hung in the back kitchen and we file into the kitchen proper, sitting down to baked beans on toast. I wonder about Dave. Was he there? In the grey world? I decide on a little test. He is sat next to me as usual. I snarl and quickly fork up his last corner of toast. He's on it, his knife dropped and grabbing my hand, including the fork. The toast pings off, describes a parabola across the kitchen table and lands with a 'plop!' in Pa's tea. Barely looking up, Pa removes the toast and inspects his mug for further contamination. Dave and I shoot a sideways glance at one another, tittering. He eats the rest of his beans off his fork, I eat mine off my knife. We hold hands like we will never let go. Mum looks on aghast: she doesn't mind the hand-holding, but eating off my knife?

Really?

LIFECHOICE

THE LACTIC ACID is building in my legs as I swing along in a rhythm established nine kilometres ago. But I can see Amanda Lee in our blue chequered strip less than a hundred metres ahead: she's an excellent swimmer and good on a bike but a way slower runner than me. I'm catching her with every stride and I know once I'm up with her I'll pass in a flash and the race will be mine. The chase is on and Amanda shoots me a tired glance as I pass. Not far now. I can hear Pete, my boyfriend of but a couple of months, cheering me on, having finished in the men's section already. Too tired to acknowledge him, I take the final bend, the finish in sight. I've won! Happy, happy, relieved. I turn to greet Amanda as she crosses the line and we fall into a sweaty hug.

"I was waiting for you to catch me, just couldn't go faster," she pants.

"Thought I'd never get to you," I lie.

The lads are with us now: Pete, Eli and Ed. We only have to wait for Penny to finish and we might be in with a chance for the mixed team prize. All the lads finished in the top 15, with Ed the best in 3rd. Penny finishes a tired 20th and we end up in 2nd. Still, I am awarded a tacky plastic trophy and a pair of socks for winning. What could be better?

Everyone seems on a high, the atmosphere buzzing. Some have booked a physio session to help them recover from their race. People are packing up their kit. Ed is back on his bike, off to cycle another 10k home, back to his wife and their twin boys. He says as soon as they are old enough they can come and watch. A bit older still and he'll have them on a bike! Eli and Pete have a roof rack on Pete's car and us girls have... my works transit. Beautifully decorated with pictures of orchids, seeing as I work in a florist's. The boxes which hold arrangements for weddings and stuff are removed and we can easily wheel in three bikes, chuck the bags in then all of us jump in up front.

I drop Amanda off first. "See you at The Dog and Gun," she calls, her bag over her shoulder, tripping over the pedal of her bike. "Steadeee," laughs Penny. We always rock up at The Dog and Gun. Chew over the race while drinking the creamy bitter and dining on the floppy, tragic sandwiches.

I'm beginning to feel stiff and chilled. "Can't wait to get into a hot bath," I groan.

"Me too," from Penny.

"Get your own bath!" We nudge each other like a couple of kids. "Get out of my van, bitch."

I push her: we are just around the corner from Amanda's house, straight to Penny's back door. A longer drive to our flat. Our flat, the one above the florists which I share with my sister. It has two bedrooms, kitchen, bathroom and lounge. Bigger than the other flats in the row as it extends further back over a sort of garage area where we prepare bouquets and larger arrangements. So relieved to see the lights off in the gathering autumn gloom, it means Emma isn't in and I can soak in the bath forever... Well, you know...

It isn't a good idea for me to eat soon after a race, gives me stomach ache. But now, sat cross-legged on my bed, brushing out my wet hair after a long soak, I'm starving. I can almost feel the cool beer going down my throat. On goes my usual outfit: jeans and a polo shirt. I add a thick fleece in view of the evening chill and patterned Doc Marten shoes. Still a bit stiff going downstairs, I lock up and with hands thrust firmly in pockets set off at a brisk walk to cover the half-mile to The Dog and Gun.

The pub is an ugly red-brick building, roadside frontage and no parking. Even so, it has plenty of regular punters and as I open the door this evening I'm met by a thick, warm fug and the sound of many conversations, joshing, laughter. Our team had ordered a sandwich buffet which comes with piles of softening crisps and 'growlers' – pork pie pieces bound to disturb the digestive process. This was served in the snug – a small room at the back of the pub. I make my way there, the last to arrive. Pete is sat at a table facing me and next to him, wouldn't you know it, is Rose. Rose the gooseberry. Rose the hanger-on. She started tailing Pete – honestly, I can think of no other way to describe it – the moment she set eyes on him. I'm amazed she wasn't cheering him on at the race today. She seems to know every move he makes and when I challenged him about it he said, "We're just mates, chill. She's not like you. You're… pure," and he kissed me and everything seemed okay. But here she is again, sitting too close to Pete and when she looks at me it's, well, smug. Ed introduced Pete to us when he moved up from Sussex and right from the first Rose had had the hots for him. She was gutted when he started going out with me, she'd do anything to split us up. Anyhows, she's not in our team so why doesn't she fly back to her perch near the bar…? Still, no one else seems to mind so perhaps I am being a bit green-eyed. And, anyway, Pete shoots me a glance which could melt ice. He's looking super-sexy in his specs – he wears contacts to race but he says they soon irritate his eyes. Squeezing between Eli and Amanda on the bench facing Pete, I help myself to a corned beef and pickle sandwich and a swig of one of the pints of bitter lined up on the table. Yum!

Turns out we would have won the team prize if Ed hadn't picked up a penalty for not taking his cycle helmet off in transition. Derr! We're giving him some stick when Rose tosses her beautiful mane of auburn hair and flutters her ever-so-long fake lashes, "Actually, guys," she wafts a manicured hand at our faces, "I have something that will make sure the team win every time." She has our attention. Fissling round in her capacious tote bag, she retrieves a gold and black glossy folder and proceeds to hand out leaflets from within it. "S'pose you better have one," she snarls at me, "we all know THAT'S a waste of paper." Nice. Ed immediately folds his into a plane and it flies into the bar area. Impressive. Perhaps Rose has waited a couple of pints too long? Anyhows, the rest of us begin to read. 'LIFECHOICE' it says across the top of the leaflet. And between the glossy pictures of people performing amazing stunts and winning medals, the paragraphs describe an implant that will 'change your life forever' and make 'all your wildest dreams attainable'. It lost me at 'implant'. I got up to refresh the beer supply and, of course, a gin for Lady Rose.

As I get back with the beers Rose is signing people up to a talk about the implant thing. Pete's going and there's no way I'm leaving him in her clutches for an evening. Much to her chagrin, mine too if I'm honest, I put my name down.

It's late, I'm tired. I get up and say goodbye and, yes!, Pete says he'll walk me home. Well maybe I'm not THAT tired! As we quit the pub the cold air hits us and I, at least, feel I have had plenty to drink. We walk side by side, my arm through his and then our hands back in pockets. The lights are still off at the flat; Emma is often on a late one on a Saturday. She works front of house at a restaurant where I couldn't afford to eat. Then she usually has the energy to hit the town.

Feel okay to invite Pete in. He follows me up the stairs to the kitchen and I flick on the kettle. "Mmm…" He is leaning on me, squashing me back on the sink. "I'm not thirsty, I'm hungry and I'm going to eat you up!"

"Get off!" I protest. But I don't mean it. Wriggling from under him, I escape to my bedroom with Pete in hot pursuit, making slobbery animal noises. We end up in a giggly heap on the bed. Pete stops and carefully puts his specs on the bedside table and just for a second I think I should clean my teeth. I always clean my teeth. But clothes are flying off…

And Pete can make love. Always fun and tender and thoughtful. Afterwards we lay on top of the quilt, legs entangled. My hand traces the line of his jaw, his handsome face beautifully shadowed in the soft light coming through the open bedroom door from the kitchen. Thank goodness tomorrow is Sunday, 'cos now we can sleep and sleep.

Only too soon I am woken by my phone ringing. It stops and then immediately starts again.

The bedroom door is still open, the kitchen light on and it's here the sound comes from.

"Leave it," Pete mumbles sleepily. But I have to answer it. It might be Emma.

I pick up. "At last," Emma, sounding relieved, "I've been ringing and ringing."

I glance at the kitchen clock. It's 4.30. "Yeh, maybe I didn't answer 'cos it's the middle of the night. Wot's happening?"

"Karen, lovely Karen, best sister evuur…"

Oh-oh! thinks I.

"I seem to have, er, lost everybody and I'm at Wakefield bus station. Pleeease can you fetch me, pleeease?"

"How. The. Hell. Can you lose everyone? Can't you find a cab?" I can't believe this. She knows I'll go get her. I know I'll go get her. Anyhows, I'm awake now and it IS Sunday.

By now Pete has shuffled into the kitchen, his blond cropped hair sticking everywhere and specs slightly awry. "You look like an electrocuted coconut," I observe, stretching my arms up and around his broad shoulders.

He wraps himself around me, mouth so close to my ear, "That," he whispers, "is no way to speak to the man who is going to drive you to Wakefield to pick up your bonkers sister." Scooping the transit keys off the work surface, I dangle them in his face. "Oh, actually it looks like you're driving the flower bus," he says. I'm just glad he's coming with.

As we leave the parade of shops I notice a shiny dark red Kia Sportage parked outside the florists. No one parks in the shop lay-by overnight. Wait a minute, isn't that Rose's car? Well creepy.

We pick up Emma then drop off Pete on the way home. Pete and I have decided to go for a jog out later, just to 'turn the legs over'. Back at the flat I make a start on bacon sandwiches, but Emma is asleep on the settee before I've even sliced the bread. I finish making the sandwiches, tomato sauce for Emma, brown for me, then eat them both. Pretty soon I'm in the armchair across from Emma joining her in slumber.

* * *

I think I'll join the winter cross-country league. I wonder if Penny and Amanda would be interested? Well, I'll know in a minute. Already it has come around to Rose's 'Lifechoice' doodah and here I am, playing taxi in the transit. I'm in my usual jeans and polo, topped with a thick coat, though when

I pick up Penny she has a long mac on, her bestest sexy boots and probably the gorgeous red dress. Unusual for her. When we get to Amanda's she teeters out in heels and a skirt that barely covers her arse.

"Where are you going?" I tease.

Penny and Amanda exchange glances. "Rose said we were off to Zinni's after the meet," says Penny. Oh, so, no invite. Not awkward at all. Can't go to posh Zinni's in jeans.

"Well I hope you've got a lift home then." From me. Cross.

I drive on to the leisure centre and the car park is already packed. Not the easiest vehicle to park. I drop my friends off and head back to the main road for a space. Do I go to the meet or not? Count to 10, out of transit, walk purposefully in, head high, smile on. Free drinks are being handed out in the foyer, orange juice or spring water. And there are canapé-type things, but they look risky, like snails! There are loads of people here that I either know or recognise. People on the triathlon circuit. Runners, some ladies from the local hockey team. I pass into the main hall looking for Pete and see him talking earnestly to a rugged-looking man alongside one of the flashy displays. Pete is looking edible in a blazer and open-neck shirt, cord trousers and suede shoes. Mr Rugged glances at his phone to check the time and directs Pete to the seats. Pete spies me, smiles and gestures me over. We sit side by side and he rests a hand on my thigh. I'm so aware of it there, wishing he would track higher. On my other side is Eli's girlfriend Serena, a big unit and no mistake, then Eli looking skinny as a rake beside her. Rose is posing about with a clipboard, getting everyone seated. The lights dim, let the show begin.

There's ethereal music. Haunting. Beautiful. On the screen pictures of big cats. Agile, strong and supple. The dialogue in a rich voice starts to outline how the implant would work for us. The hall is warm, my chair comfortable... crikey, I am struggling to keep my eyes open. I feel like I need matchsticks. Then the tempo changes and the film starts to focus on individuals already using Lifechoice. It's a big screen and the camera work is amazing, I feel like I'm flying off with the base jumpers... AIIIEE! Then there are street dancers, showing incredible moves, bouncing all over. We switch to climbing and there's a guy dangling confidently by one hand over a fearful precipice, not a rope in sight. The film explains that Lifechoice is relatively new to athletics with new programs: Cheetah for speed and Wolf for endurance. A powerful-looking man is shown breezing a 5000m steeplechase, finishing barely out of breath. The lights come up and Mr Rugged introduces himself as Pablo. Lifechoice, he says, holding a tiny cylinder between forefinger and thumb, is an implant which sits at the base of the skull adjacent to the cervical vertebrae. Simple to insert, it would then send out connections resembling a fungal mycelium to connect directly to the spine.

Controlled by an app, either on your PC or mobile, you can program your own development. You can work to improve your VO2 max, your muscle mass. The implant monitors all of your vital signs so it is easy to track your progress. The presentation was slick. Convincing.

There is applause. Next, Rose and Pablo are fielding questions. Of course you can remove it. Look on it as a symbiant... The price, they say, depends on which program you choose. Questions over, Rose, and Pablo with, start to come round with clipboards. They are signing people up for the implant and it looks like the uptake is good. I wander over to one of the displays and pick up an implant. It looks innocuous enough. Still, I trust my own training programme: after all, I am winning. I know I need to improve my swimming – no need for an implant to tell me that.

Suddenly I'm aware of Rose at my shoulder. "You can't afford it," she snaps.

I pass her the implant and stomp off to find Amanda and Penny. Amanda says she is going to give the transplant a go. "Why not? I need something to get me to focus, make me turn out to train in the rain," she says.

"Ha!" Penny puffs, shaking her head, "Who doesn't? And I should stop quaffing beer and stuffing my face with cake, but I like cake! The exercise is just to make me feel better about the bad eating habits."

"Are we ready to go?" Crikey, it's Rose again, When did she creep up? Pete isn't far behind her. "Er, actually," says Pete, taking in my casual attire, "Karen and I have other plans. Sorry, Rose."

"Ooh! Where are you twos off to?" asks Pen.

"We," Pete, slightly behind me, slaps a hand onto each of my shoulders, grips and gives me a shake, "are going to Turner's." Turner's, the chippy on the high street. Ideal.

Penny's eyes light up. "Curry sauce AND mushy peas?" I can see her binning off Zinni's.

"The table is booked." Rose stares at Pen Very Hard. "And, Penny," more softly, "you look lovely, you wouldn't want to waste that look on a fish shop."

Actually, Penny looks uncomfortable: the skirt keeps riding up her bum and she could break an ankle if she wobbles off the heels. But here's Eli and Serena. "Fish and chips?" cheerily, from Serena. "Great idea, then everyone back to ours!"

As Amanda and Penny walk back to the transit with me I can't help but feel bad about Rose. Does she think I deliberately set out to ruin her plans? I never would have. It's up to Serena to invite her along as well, isn't it? It's their house. Anyway, we're on the fish and chips order, Pete is fetching beer, Serena and Eli are warming the plates.

Once we are all together the conversation is all about Lifechoice. Pete has actually signed up for a double implant, Wolf and Tiger. Then he drops another bombshell into the conversation,

"I like," he says, "the planned termination option."

"What, like you decide what age you're going to die?" Penny voices the same shock as I feel.

"Nooo!" Pete explains: "Like, if you get dementia, or if you have a bad accident, it turns you off, ceases brain function."

There's "No way!" and "What?" from those of us who aren't having an implant. This feature was not in either film or leaflet.

"Well I'd hate to be a burden to anyone. Hate to live like a vegetable never knowing the time of day. There's no way I could be in a wheelchair either, I need to be active," says young, fit, strong Pete.

"You can be active in a wheelchair…" starts Serena.

The conversation seems to go on around me and without me. I'm lost in my own thoughts.

How can you make a choice like that now? Is there any chance at all that Pete could be talked out of it?

* * *

Less than a week later we're laid in bed, listening to the rain bouncing off the window, I'm running a hand down the back of Pete's neck and I feel a slight lump. "The implant," I say to myself as much as to him.

"Yeh, had it done on Monday. Rose phoned and said there was an appointment available."

"Where did you go? Did it hurt?"

"It was at the Penguin hotel, just a room there, some bloke in a white coat and surgical gloves. Took a second... Itches a bit now, like."

I'm taken aback. I thought he would have time to think about it. Now it's too late. "Does it make you feel different?" I ask.

"No, but look at this." He reaches to the bedside table, picking up specs first and propping them on his nose before flicking through to the Lifechoice app on his phone. "Every breath, heartbeat, my maintenance energy requirement. Look, I can have a bun for the energy expended with having sex!"

Having sex. Talk about objectifying something. "Is this recorded somewhere?" I have visions of Rose sat at some PC noting frequency and duration of our most intimate moments.

"Chill, Karen," said so softly; "Karen," a whisper. And I sink into his kisses.

* * *

The first race of the Winter Cross-Country league is on ings land alongside the River Wharfe. As usual the programme starts with the juniors, then the intermediate and my ladies' race is the penultimate start, senior men going last. The course is pretty level being alongside the river but very muddy and even flooded in places. For us ladies there are three laps to run. Six muddy miles. I'm feeling in good form, carefully tying on my studs. One thing running with wet feet, quite another losing your shoes. Time to strip down to my shorts, always the worst bit as the raw wind claws at my bare legs. There are about 20 in the ladies' race and of course I know many of them, by sight if not by name. There's Amanda here for a start. However, I like to keep myself to myself, find my zone. As we line up I'm thinking about my race, working my gloves right to the base of my fingers. I'm nervous. Pocklington AC are shouting for someone called Christine. "Come on, Christine." "Go Christine." Don't know her, must be fancied. We are started by a whistle and everyone shoots off, getting a position before the path narrows alongside the river. Christine has taken the lead, there's a couple more ladies then, much to my amazement, it's Amanda, two more souls then myself. Amanda is usually a way behind me. I'm not worried, there's plenty of time for me to make up ground. At the far end of the course we turn off the river bank, through a gate into heavy plough. My skinny legs and slight build make light work of the heavy going; I feel light and strong. By the end of the plough there are only Christine, Amanda and one other ahead. I am beginning to gain on Amanda.

It's the final lap, time to make my move. Amanda and I are in second and third place respectively and Christine is coming back to us. I pass Amanda, but she's rallying, sticking to my shoulder. We pass the weakening Christine as one. My breathing has become harsh, my legs feel like they're taking extra-long jelly strides. At last, with a couple hundred yards to run, Amanda gives way. I practically fall over the line, mud-splattered and knackered. Bending over, hands on knees, gasping to pay back my oxygen debt. I really had to try. Amanda joins me, thumping my back. "Still can't beat you!" she pants. She has certainly improved. A lot.

It's bliss to work thick woolly socks over my wet, muddy feet, pull on fleecy leggings and my thick jacket. Amanda and I watch the men's race together. Amanda waves to someone – oh! It's Rose. What joy. Pete's running. Finally, as the rain begins to fall ever so heavy, Pete finishes third. The first nine home, Rose observes, have all signed up to Lifechoice.

* * *

"So what's the point?" I start in The Dog and Gun later that day. "If everybody signs up to Lifechoice, you lose your advantage."

"I've never been in the top three in cross-country in my life," says Pete. "It makes me a competitor rather than an also-ran. Anyway, I'm beginning to feel altogether better now."

"Yeh, but you're also training harder. Don't you think that's what's made the difference?"

"Doesn't matter if it is, I'm getting the results." Pete is bullish.

Okay, fair play.

All the usual crowd are there, including Rose. I haven't seen Eli for ages and wonder what he is up to. "Keeping fit?" I ask him.

"Yeh, I'm doing a lot more in the gym, bulking up a bit. I've joined a rock-climbing club and it's great fun. Don't know why I've never done it before. We've been to The Chevin today, on the granite."

"What you have, monkey implant?" A dig from Pen.

"Arctic monkey in this weather," I add.

"There isn't a monkey implant," snaps Rose. Defensive "Oo-oo-oo!" from everyone.

"Do you have an implant, Rose?" Reasonable question, surely, from Amanda.

"Don't be silly, I'm a marketing executive."

"Promotion from Brad's Kebabs, anyroad." It's unlike Amanda to be snide, but, get in! Now I think about it, I can remember Rose there. She doesn't look the same without the bright green uniform.

"Bet I can climb as well as you," challenges Pete.

"We need a race," says Rose. "How about over the bridge and first one to the top of the lamp post, far side, wins?"

"Naked," adds Amanda.

"You're on!" Pete jumps up and heads for the door.

The rain has turned to sleet and it's bitter cold. Still, as we all walk down the hill to the west end of the river bridge, Eli and Pete are shedding clothes. Pete's specs fall on the pavement; I collect them up and pop them in my pocket. There are four lampposts across the long bridge, glowing yellow through the sludgy night. Rose is really into this, she's acting as starter. It's bonkers: it's not that late and there's a fair passage of traffic passing over the bridge. A couple walking the other way see us and cross sides, walking briskly.

"Aaand, on three, one... two... GO!" laughs Rose. Ed, Amanda, Penny all shouting. Me wishing the pavement would swallow me up. Pete and Eli are pushing and grabbing at each other, Eli's on his knees, he's got Pete by the ankle. They're both down. They're both up. Pete gets a run on Eli and makes the fourth lamppost in the lead and starts to climb. But Eli is close behind and really is like a rat up a drainpipe, soon grabbing at Pete's ankles. Clinging on, Pete finally makes the light at the top. Cheers from everyone, including me as hopefully now we can all settle down before someone is arrested. Pete and Eli half-slide, half-fall to the ground. Both are badly grazed.

"Pete, are you okay?" I ask when I reach him, trying to cover him up, wrapping his coat around his shoulders.

"You really are a boring cow, aren't you?" Rose has a handful of my hair and she pulls my face towards hers. "Pete will wake up and see the light soon."

Pete pulls on his trousers and throws his coat over his shoulders. "Come on, let's go back to yours." It sounds like a command, he has an urgency about him. The others are drifting back to The Dog and Gun so I call my goodbyes. Pete route-marches on. He hasn't bothered with his socks or shoes so his feet must be frozen.

Soon we are at the flat and as soon as I shut the street door behind us Pete is all over me. What is this? Sweaty frenzy time? I half-expected him to revert to normal, crack a smile and lead me up the stairs. I feel like lightening the mood, but I'm guessing he's deadly earnest. Still, there is no way I'm getting bucked in the stairwell. I manage to detach his face from mine. "Not here, upstairs." He nods obediently and bounds up the stairs, dragging me by the hand. Seeing as it's Sunday I know Emma will be in. Sure enough, she's draped over the settee watching some crime thing on TV. I give her a 'help me' look. She gives a 'rather you than me' look in return and turns the volume up.

I try to join in with the rampant sex thing, but I'm not feeling it. One thing is absolutely certain, Pete doesn't notice. In fact he's all up for an action replay. "Hey, hey, steady, tiger." I've had enough of the rough stuff. Maybe I am as boring as Rose says. Pete actually looks at me properly. It's weird, really, 'cos without his glasses he usually squints a bit, but now I'm held by his blue eyes, the pupils dilated. He smiles: "This one is for you, gorgeous." Oh, Pete!

* * *

Holy cow, I'm cold! I've just woken up and the duvet is on the floor. A glance at the clock says it's 5.20. Nearly time to get up anyway. Flick on the bedside light: Pete is restless and his face looks strained, like he's having a bad dream. There are beads of sweat on his forehead, smudges of blood on the pillow and sheets from his grazes. I walk round the bed and throw the duvet over him, tucking him in. Time to sort some warm clothes. If I have used the transit the day before

I usually go to the flower market in Leeds. This means I almost invariably go on a Monday. My boss, the owner of the shop, my co-worker and friend Margaret, goes the rest of the time. Many of the flowers are delivered direct from Holland. Margaret and I get on really well and I have much to learn from her; she seems to just throw an arrangement together yet the balance is always spot on, the colours perfect. I need to sort myself a flask and a bite of breakfast. I'm eating my frosted flakes when Pete dashes out of the bedroom, throwing on clothes nearly as fast as he took them off last night.

"Why didn't you wake me?" he asks. "I need to get a ten-miler in this morning, busy at work, no time later." He's heading for the door, halts, spins, strides back to me and kisses my cheek.

"I'm going in a mo, have a lift." I say with mouth full. So he swipes the spoon and takes the biggest possible mouthful of flakes. Just helping me finish my breakfast, then.

I'm looking forward to the market. I realise I'm boring Peter with going on about it. He's not listening, anyhows. He looks tense like he's about to race, never mind a train-ing run. And why so far after yesterday's cross-country? As we get to his place he waves and jogs up to the door of the pretty little semi. Bye, Pete! It's only when I get to the market I realise I still have his glasses in my pocket. He has plenty of spares but these are his favourite pair. I text him to let him know where they are.

We start making wreaths for Christmas today and we need teasels, faux holly and ivy and the frames to put them on. I can spend any quiet time in the shop spraying fir cones with gold or silver spray or that fake snow stuff. Then they are attached to florists' wire. As well as the flowers we sell greetings cards, planters and vases and locally made garden ornaments. Then Margaret and I are helping out with the decor of 'Winter Wonderland' set up at Woodend Nurseries. It's great fun, Margaret has done a fantastic birch sculpture of a reindeer. Training will have to fit in around the work. I'll be spending the time in the gym. No running in the frost and dark for me.

* * *

It's been all tinsel, baubles and teasels! It feels like I haven't seen Pete for a lifetime when he collects me for our next cross-country race. This venue starts at the base of Sutton Bank. There is a steep climb across pasture land, then you travel along the top of the bank for nearly a mile. Beautiful views over the Vale of York. The route then dips down through woodland, including crossing a stream, before more fields to the finish. It's around eight miles and the only race in the series where everyone runs together. It's a bright frosty day and my legs feel light and springy. Everyone is on the line, the starting horn gives a loud 'PARP' and there is a mad dash, jostling and pushing, as the field fights for a possie before the gate into the first field. As it's a mixed field it's harder to keep tabs on other senior ladies. I can see Amanda Lee up ahead (surely she has set off too fast?) and sort of feel Christine behind. She must be pacing herself using me. I really enjoy the run, apart from the stream bit; it's way too deep if you ask me – frozen feet for the rest of the way! The next time I see Amanda, she is, as I am, running downhill; one more field to the finish. She is crossing the line, her blonde ponytail swizzling round on top of her head. I'm sure she's upsides Ed, so that's some run.

"Aaaow!" escapes involuntarily from my lips as I trip over a tree root. Probably should look where I'm going, then!

Christine is directly behind me, "You OK?" she asks as I get off my knees.

"Hey, yes thanks. Too busy watching the finish."

"Oh, yeh, the implant gang. It'll end in tears."

We run on together, finishing in equal ninth.

The gang are there to cheer me over the line. Get this – I am the last of us to finish. Ed is a bit miffed to be beaten by Pete and Eli. Still, we all agree to meet at The Dog and Gun later for the usual beer and sarnies.

* * *

I wanted to see a bit more of Pete this week so he's invited me to go swimming this evening. I know I really need to work on my swimming so I agree to the Monday night, adult-lane swim. I've already put my one-piece costume on and stuff knickers, goggles and little rubbery hat along with a towel and shower gel into a bag for life. The bus to town stops outside our parade of shops and after a hundred (feels like) stops I descend near the pool. It's a short transition from the warm bus through the evening chill into the toasty heat of the foyer where I wait for Pete. He's soon in sight, jogging with a rucksack on. I hand over my cash, Pete flashes his loyalty card.

As I'm ready dressed I make the pool before Pete and ease myself into the water – *Brr!* – wet my goggles and start to put them on carefully over the hat. My hair is plaited and the plait pulled up over my head, I don't want to move it. Pete emerges from the changing rooms in a tiny pair of budgie-smugglers. He looks like an extreme body builder without the tan. His head looks too small for his body. If I wasn't going out with him already I wouldn't give him a second look. He had a good body before, perfect, and this is… ugly.

He dives in, barely raising a ripple, and off he swims. It's a 25m pool so I decide to do 60 lengths. As I keep forgetting my count I add on lengths rather than shortening the swim. After sort of 60, I've had enough. I wait for Pete at the pool end and accost him as he turns to let him know I'm getting out. He gives me a thumbs-up and pushes off for more lengths.

I've taken my time showering and now I'm on the balcony watching the flow of the swimmers. I chose a latte and a packet of cheese and onion from the machines. Up and down goes Pete. The good news is he'll have to come out before 10. The bad news is, he looks like he's going to take it all the way to the wire.

I do a bit of Facebook time, text Pen, my Mum, Amanda and finally Emma. Monday is another night off for Emma and she's delighted I'm still out and about. Unlike me she has wheels, a cream-coloured mini. She suggests she pick us up and we drop in at Turner's. She's at the pool before Pete makes it up to the gallery. More people are arriving to swim and we watch them. At last Pete is with us.

"We're going to Turner's for tea," states Emma. It's a done deal. Pete flicks across the screen of his phone and after a heartbeat – "Okay, Lifechoice says I can have fish." Good old Lifechoice.

Emma is in the car outside, engine running, Pete and I go into the shop where the rotund Mrs Turner is serving and her six-foot-five son cooking. I don't think Pete would take him on even now. "Three fish, two chips and curry sauce, please." I'm so hungry.

"Chips!" Pete snorts. "When I looked up at you on the balcony you were stuffing your face with crisps!"

"A little teeny-weeny packet after all that swimming."

"Ha! You were only in the pool five minutes, no wonder you're losing your form."

Mrs Turner shot him a disparaging glare. Raising one side of her mono-brow she loaded up her chip scoop to full capacity and, as she wrapped the order, "Put some scraps in there for you as well, lovey."

"Mint, thanks!"

Back at the flat Emma and I prepare to dig into our portions out of the paper. Pete gets out a plate, knife and fork and commences to pick batter off his fish. "Got any scales?" he asks.

Well, we just sit there like a couple of dopes: like, is it that the fish has scales? Does he mean bones? "S-c-a-l-e-s. To weigh the fish." Pete looks exasperated.

"N-o." What's wrong with him, it's A Portion Of Fish.

Emma smirks.

We eat in silence, well not talking anyway. Pete finishes before us. Well, we have way more to go at. Then he gets his phone out again. "I need seven hours of sleep," he announces and with that goes into my bedroom and shuts the door.

"What the –?" Emma laughs. We shake our heads. Honestly, help yourself Pete.

"Pass the sauce, Em."

When I retire, Pete is fast asleep. As before, it isn't restful, his muscles jumping and twitching, face tense. Luckily I'm so tired I sleep regardless of his restlessness.

* * *

I'm looking forward to this evening. Pete is taking me to the 'Winter Wonderland' that Margaret and I helped decorate. Can't wait to show him our grotto and the illuminated langlauf trail. The skating rink will be open, too. Margaret has given Pete her free entry ticket, we can skate ourselves silly.

Pete is in a festive mood, wearing jeans, boots and a wool coat along with scarf and a woolly hat with a ridiculous pom-pom. I have a bright pink padded jacket on with jeans and fleece-lined boots. I'm not sure which of us is worse at skating. Pete falls over more 'cos he's trying to go too fast too soon. I think I'm actually better going backwards. As the rink fills with families we head off to the langlauf. Just as I think I've cracked it we reach an uphill bit and I start sliding backwards. Pete extends a ski pole to pull me up. Instead he is pulled down and we end up falling into the hedge tangled up with our skis. Small children ski confidently past.

Skis deposited back at the hire barn, we go dine on mince pies with brandy butter and lattes.

Pete has been like Pete. He hasn't checked in with Lifechoice once. The flat feels toasty warm when we get back. Coats are hung in the stairwell and I go into my bedroom for slippers. Pete follows me in. He pushes me firmly onto the bed. He's pulling at the buttons on my jeans. "Hey, steady!" I try to hold his hands but he pushes me back on the bed. My jeans are at half-mast and he holds me down, his right forearm across my breastbone, his left holding my head back by my plait. He manoeuvres his knee between my thighs, then the other knee forceful and strong, then he pushes himself into me. His head is beside mine so I am unable to see his face. A couple of thrusts later and he's done. I just lay there, feeling violated, used. I don't want it to, but a tear rolls out my eye and tracks down to my ear.

Pete rolls off and props himself up on one elbow. He looks at me, snorts. "For goodness sake, Karen, I can't always be waiting for you!"

He pulls up his jeans and I hear him in the kitchen getting a glass of water. Then to the bathroom where he locks the door and I hear the shower begin to run. Turn onto my belly, wipe my eyes with the heel of my hand. I spy his mobile on the bedside table and caterpillar across the bed to reach it. There's no lock on the phone so I decide to check in with Lifechoice. And, guess what? It says Pete should have sex this evening, to 'de-stress'. And this coming Saturday.

Now I'm mad. I'm not part of some program! Just then, in comes Pete. Looks at me. Looks at the phone. "Karen, what's happening here?"

"Well you're not. Get out." He looks crushed. "GET OUT!" I throw the phone at him and it hits him in the chest. He catches it deftly before it hits the floor.

"Karen, please, no. You can't."

He's actually crying and then he falls to his knees, hands on the edge of the bed.

"Karen, don't. You're important... You know, for everything." Then he said it. "Lifechoice."

Not 'I love you', then. Bastard! I hit him with a pillow first, then a teddy. "Go away. Stay away... Pig!"

Once I get hold of the bedside lamp the penny drops and he's offski. The lamp falls short of the door, held by its cable. He must have gone down the stairs in two bounds. I hear the front door slam and the engine of his car start. Sitting up I give way to tears and, seeing his shoes by the bed, grab them and chuck them out the window.

* * *

It's not like we've been going out long, but I miss Pete, old Pete, and I think about him a lot. Now we are in December there is loads to do. Work, training, shopping. Pen, Amanda and I have a girls' night out. I go out with Emma and Mum.

Still, Pete creeps into my thoughts. One freezy afternoon I decide on a run that just so happens to pass his house. As it's cold I need to put on a couple of layers and a fleece hat just to get out the door so by the time I pass his house I'm mafted. Just have to slow down a tiddly bit while I put the hat in my pocket. Of course Rose's car is in the drive, why wouldn't it be? I think I see a curtain twitch so I'm on my way, a lump in my throat, a weird feeling in my chest.

* * *

I can't remember the last time I drove to a race all by my little self. This will be the last of the cross-country series before Christmas. Up near Knaresborough there's a mixture of road, track and field involved so studs are out and there's ample opportunity to slide about in the mud. Lasses run first, then the lads. As I hop about trying to get my tracksuit bottoms over my trainers without pasting everything in the meltwater behind the transit, Pete and Rose saunter by arm in arm. She gives me a cool stare and nudges Pete. The look he shoots me is absolutely bloody. He whispers something to Rose and she hoots with laughter. I drop my tracksuit leg in the mud.

Amanda comes up to greet me. "You're running late," she says. "See our Rose soon got her claws into Pete." Not wanting to talk about it, I turn the conversation round to the race. You know, is she fit and that.

I'm glad when we get going. It's an absolutely freezing day, white all over and a blue, blue sky. We crunch along bunched at a good pace up along the first track before climbing into pasture land. Many of the fences are stock wire but there are stone walls too. The grass is slippery and it drags the energy out of you keeping your feet. Soon Amanda breaks away from our lead group. By the time she reaches one of the many stiles we have to cross she is a good twenty metres ahead. The stile is a sort of A-shaped ladder affair over a stone wall. Amanda ascends, then slips at the top. Off balance, she sort of stalls in mid-stride, arms flailing, then headplants over the other side of the wall. It's well comical, it's giving us all a right laugh.

A couple of us climb carefully over the style and Amanda is laid out on the other side. It's horrible to see. Her head is thrown back, eyes rolled back into her skull as she claws at the frosted grass and nettle at the base of the wall like she is having some kind of fit. All the while she's groaning and whining.

"Get her into the recovery position," Christine takes charge. "Karen, go and alert the ambulance."

It's like waking out of a trance, one second staring bog-eyed at Amanda, now having something useful to do. St Johns Ambulance are always at the meet. Glad not to have to watch Amanda so distressed, I race back to the start as fast as I can.

The race is halted, the later contests cancelled. I can't understand how Amanda can be so badly hurt. It was a slow fall over a few feet onto grass. There was no blood anywhere, no gaping head wound. But by the time she is stretchered back to the ambulance she is deathly still, lips blue, face white.

I head to Harrogate District Hospital to see if I can get any news of Amanda at A&E. The dragon on reception states she can only give information to a relative. Then I see Christine walking away from the patient assessment area. Someone calls her back: "Dr Kelling…".

Aha, a doctor. I wait for her to reappear. "Christine, sorry to butt in."

"I know, your friend, I'm so sorry."

Christine could give no explanation for Amanda's passing. Perhaps it was a bleed on the brain? The post-mortem would show. Despondent, I drive home.

* * *

Four days later and Margaret and I are taking orders for Christmas flowers and selling our gift selection like there's no tomorrow. I'm just selling a bloke a lovely coloured glass vase when I see Serena enter the shop. She mooches around the greetings cards. As soon as I'm free I bounce over, pleased to see her. As she turns I see she is pregnant, her coat not quite covering her bump.

"Hey, congratulations! You've been keeping that quiet!"

Serena bursts into tears, launching towards me in an awkward hug on account of the bump. Sobs rack her body. Signalling to Margaret, I steer Serena to our preparation area out the back of the shop.

"What's wrong, darling? Hey?"

"Eli, it's Eli. He's been k-killed climbing," Serena manages to get out between sobs. I pass her a tissue but she uses her cuff anyway. Plonking herself down on a plastic chair, she seems to become calmer.

"It's awful," she starts, "too awful. He went to do some ice climbing with Ben and Sticks." (Don't know them but didn't want to interrupt.) "They were doing a relatively easy section up a gully on the North Face of Ben Nevis. Eli was climbing last and a piton came loose and he fell. Sticks said it wasn't a long fall and they called down to see if he was okay. Apparently he shouted back that he'd had a bump but was just sorting out his ropes and he'd be ready to climb. That was the last they heard. Sticks could just see him and he said Eli just crumpled up. By the time they abseiled down to him he was dead."

First Amanda, now Eli. Within a week. As I hold Serena's hand I just feel hollow.

* * *

The Sunday before Christmas. I'm sitting in our lounge on the arm of the settee, staring out at the sodden street below. It's been dull all day and it seems it got dark at two. A blustery wind chases scraps of paper up the street outside, a sheet of newspaper making the height of our window. Then it swirls off, lodging itself in the gutter of one of the houses opposite. Someone has gone into the general store two doors down and left their little Westie tied to one of the flower troughs. It crouches miserably as far out of the wind as it can get, cold despite its fluorescent coat. The scene looks like I feel.

Amanda's funeral won't be until the new year and Eli will stay forever in Scotland. It's where his folks are from.

Emma emerges from the bathroom, towelling her blond hair. My little sister, an inch taller than me and a stronger build. She takes after Dad; I'm small and dark like Mum.

"Get ready, you," she says. "You're not skulking away in here."

"I really don't want to go out. I'm in a skulky mood."

In the end I agree to let her drag me down to The Dog and Gun. I don't have to get changed and I fancy a bit of a walk.

As usual, the grotty little pub is packed. We weave our way to the bar and, you'd never guess what... Rose is serving! "Evening ladies!" she smiles. Actually smiles. As always there is the rich curtain of auburn hair and the thick coating of slap, but neither can fully conceal the bruising down the side of her face. Emma orders a half of cider and I order a pint.

"On me!" says Rose.

"Really?" I'm genuinely incredulous. "Thanks. Eerm, dare I ask, what happened to the Lifechoice job?"

Rose waves a well-manicured hand dismissively. "Oh, it was going nowhere, you know, some problems with production and they moved headquarters to South Africa... Any crisps? Sandwiches?" Rose turns to another punter, takes the order for his pint and starts to fill the glass. Then to me, leaning closer: "And that Pete, thought he'd be a good guy, you know, seemed a sweetheart, but, hey, what a vicious bastard!"

We took our drinks and squidged onto a table with a couple of gadges, they both must be deaf as posts 'cos they're shouting to each other 'bout the football.

* * *

I feel like I haven't slept a wink then, just as I feel real sleepy, the alarm goes off. Monday at the flower market and we need loads of flowers for Christmas. Here I am in the kitchen making a flask to take with me, trying to down frosted flakes at high speed, when Emma wanders in. She looks a sight: hair everywhere, make-up still on and smudged. "I feel terrible," she snuffles, "think I'm coming down with something. I'm hot, then I'm cold..." She grabs a mug, inspects it, then proceeds to make a hot chocolate.

"Gotta go, soz. I'll see you later. Help yourself to my hot water bottle," I say. She nods sleepily, leaning back on the kitchen units and sipping her chocolate.

I need to organise the boxes in the back of the transit. Internal lights come on as I open the rear doors. I'm checking our bucket of tools hung on the side. Then, *Whump!* I'm on the floor of the transit; something big has jumped on me. I feel adrenalin burn across my chest and I wriggle and kick with all my strength. "Emma! Emma!" I shout at the top of my voice. I hope she is in her bedroom overlooking the yard and not still in the kitchen.

"Shut up, you bitch! It's all your fault. You left the program." Bloody hell, it's Pete and he's gone bonkers! I'm face down with him kneeling on my back and he's way bigger and stronger than me. He manages to pull down our tool bucket and pretty soon he's put a wrap of duct tape around my head, covering my mouth. Despite writhing around as much as possible, first one wrist, then the other is cable-tied to the D-rings in the floor of the transit, there to secure a load, not a Karen. Then Pete starts giggling. "I'm gonna make you into a vase. Something festive, hey, darling? Some holly up your arse?" Giggle.

He's found the pinking shears and he's chewing away at my belt with them while sitting on my legs. My hands are in agony, the cable ties have pulled so tight. He's cut through the waistband of my jeans and pulls them down, along with my thong over my bum. He tips the contents of the tool bucket out on the floor next to me and sniggers. I jump and writhe with the shock of him stapling a label to my arse cheek. Ow! Luckily the staple gun jams after three staples. I can hear Pete trying to pull the stuck staples out then he snorts and chucks the gun at me. I feel the smart of its impact just above my ear. My hands hurt more than ever. Pete has one foot on my back, now he is looking through the boxes for something. Not the teasels, please!

Whump! The sound of a vase on a skull. Pete falls on top of me. Emma! Oh, thank you!

"Karen, I heard you, you okay?" Emma rips the duct tape off and takes some of my hair and the skin on my lips. Youch. I run my tongue over their stinging surface and taste blood.

"There's a Stanley knife in that bucket..." I nod my head at our tool bucket. With great difficulty and only cutting me once, Emma frees me from the D-rings. I rub my wrists and wring my hands to get the circulation back, then carefully remove the label before pulling up my trousers.

"Oh hell, Karen, I think I've killed him." Emma studies Pete as I kick him off my legs. He certainly don't look great. Then his eyes roll back into his skull and his hands began to claw the side of the transit.

Then it came to me. "It's the implant, Em. It shuts them down. We've got to get them out." I grab the Stanley knife and Emma holds Pete as still as she can, sitting on him and pinning his head. The sharp blade easily cuts the skin of Pete's neck and I can see both implants. A quick dig through the bucket yields some long-nosed pliers and I tweeze the first of the implants. It takes some pulling and as it comes away there are little strands, fine as cobweb, stretching into Pete's spine. As the filaments pull clear Pete slumps lifeless to the floor of the transit. By now the second implant is slippy with blood but at last I get a decent purchase. As it comes away Pete heaves in a massive gasp of air, then his breathing becomes steadier. He's still out of it, though, his eyes half-open and glazed.

Emma races into the flat for a quilt and pillows seeing as Pete has rocked up in jeans and a T-shirt. And bare feet. Again. I call an ambulance and then Margaret. I hope she'll do the market for me.

I travel with Pete to the hospital where he is whisked into resuss and I am herded to a family room. I pace up and down for an age after which a kind nurse directs me to Pete's bedside. His breathing and heart rate are being monitored but there are no scary tubes, just a light bandage around his head. A hassled-looking doctor comes in. I tell him I am Pete's partner and he explains Pete has had a slight bleed to the brain, he is under sedation. Only time will tell if there is any brain damage or any motor damage from the removal of the implants.

I pull up a chair and rest my elbows on the bed, head on hands, looking at Pete. For the first time since he had the implant, Pete looks peaceful and relaxed.

* * *

Pete is doing really well. With the payout we got from 'Lifechoice' we have put in a stairlift so he can access all of his house, altered the bathroom and kitchen and bought a wheelchair-friendly car. I have moved in with Pete and Emma has moved François, the extremely tasty sous chef, into the flat. There has been massive media coverage about 'Lifechoice' and the lives it has affected, good or bad. The double implant was found to cause emotional instability and paranoia. On the flip side it has helped some people with spinal injuries. Pete is back at work. No longer able to handle a job in sales due to the speech problem, he's now in logistics. I know he gets frustrated by it; he knows what he wants to say but can't find the words. He is determined to walk again and I believe he will as he is both determined and brave. Already he can stand unaided. Today we are trying out a new wheelchair at St Aiden's, along the paths of the nature reserve. It has hand levers and all terrain tyres so Pete is flying along. I have to jog to keep up… it even goes up little steps. Pete pulls over next to a bench overlooking one of the lakes. Everything is starting to grow in the warm spring air. There are ducklings, trying to dive like their parents, but, too buoyant in their down coats, they bob back up like corks. Unhitching the bag from the back of the wheelchair, I get out flask and cake.

"I think," Pete says carefully, "we should get a dog."

MONSTER IN THE WOOD

PADDY NOLAN THOUGHT he'd never see the back of the grey mare. Oh, to be sure, she was a beautiful thing, dapple-grey with a silver-white mane and tail and a little pink snip on her nose. He'd taken her in a part exchange for a good coloured cob thinking he'd make a decent profit on her; his lad could sort any horse. True enough, she'd bucked and spun and reared, the bitch, but Connor sat tight and neat. Then he'd taken hold of her head and ridden her and she had obeyed sullenly, radiating ill-will with her head high and her ears flat back. Not a picture that would sell a horse. The few who had tried her had been unable to sit the bucks, had hit the deck and walked away. Now he shoved her in a stable and told Connor to prepare Dandy Man, a solid type in every way, nice bright bay with a blaze down his handsome nose and two white socks. A customer was coming to try him.

Exactly on time, Sadie Gresham-Smith decanted from her Porsche Cayenne wearing immaculate Spanish-style riding boots, cream jodhpurs and a tan suede jacket. Paddy smiled to himself. 'Ker-ching!' he thought. He greeted Sadie effusively. Did she find them alright? How was her journey? From Reading, wasn't it? Yes and yes and yes – get them saying yes! Sadie was presented with Dandy Man and was immediately disappointed. Oh, he fit the description in the paper, but he looked such a big heavy plod for a lady who would weigh eight stone wet through. A docile beast standing with his lower lip hanging loose like an old carthorse. Connor led him to the outdoor school and legged Sadie up. She felt feather-light. Paddy and Connor watched Sadie put Dandy through his paces for the next 15 minutes. No doubt about it, this girl could ride. Dandy, lazy as he was, obeyed every ask (especially "Whoa!") like an old riding-school pony. Sadie liked him even less. She dismounted, sighing. "Would you have anything else I could look at?"

Connor set off to put Dandy away and Paddy was thinking of an ex-racehorse which might fit when Sadie spotted the grey mare. "Ooh, who's that?" she enthused. "Hello, baby girl," she cooed over the mare. "Can I try her?"

Well, she could ride so with the warning that she could 'throw a buck now and again'.

Paddy fetched the tack himself. No one was missing this: Connor and the yard girls Mel and Sue, all at the side of the school. Paddy legged Sadie on. The mare raised her head high, ready to rear. Sadie let her reins slack and squeezed with her legs. Right then, thought the mare, buck not rear! And buck she did. Sadie set her weight back and sat tight and as the mare began to tire she rode her on, her rein light and her leg strong. Quietly she turned and circled the mare, slower here, faster there, turn and turn again. The horse had to concentrate hard. The commands became softer and softer, the mare flicking her ears back and forth, listening to her rider, until they floated around the school as if joined together, a single entity.

Paddy was delighted. A horse that was going to earn him a couple hundred pounds for meat an hour ago was now going to bring in several thousand. Sadie pulled the mare up and dismounted, beaming from ear to ear. "I am very interested in this one," she said, "What sort of price were you thinking?".

"Well, now," says Paddy, "look, this here's a talented harse so she is, I couldn't part with her for less than eight thousand."

Mel gasped audibly, Connor had to cover his mouth to hide the laugh that played on his lips. Though £ 8,000 was well within budget for Sadie, she was no mug. "Four, subject to vet," she replied.

"Seven, and that's as low as I can go," sighs Paddy, looking like it was breaking his heart.

"Such a shame. Just when I find a nice sort she's beyond budget, out of reach, my husband will never agree... He said six, I dare not go more than that." Sadie twisted the reins in her hand and lovingly rubbed the mare's forehead.

Throwing up his hands Paddy shakes his head in defeat. "I'm always weak when there's a lady involved, six it is."

Hands were shaken. The deal done. Everyone happy. "By the way," asks Sadie, "what is her name?"

In truth, Paddy hadn't a clue. The passport she came with had been put in the drawer with all the rest and she had been referred to as 'that grey mare'. So he said the first thing that came into his head. "Teena, we call her Teena." His grandmother's name.

Within a week, having passed veterinary inspection with flying colours, Teena was collected by Mrs Beasley, proprietor of Tang Hall Livery. This stout, middle-aged lady ran a tight ship, a well-run and successful yard equipped with everything the competitive rider needed. There was the large, airy American barn to house the sleek equine inmates, indoor and outdoor schools, a walker and a horsey solarium, not to mention tidy turnout paddocks and the professional and friendly staff.

Teena stepped off the box and went into panic mode: too much going on, too many horses, too much noise. The brightly lit barn with chattering girls, the metallic clang of the sliding doors. Then the lights stayed on well into the winter evening as owners came to ride their horses after work. And then they piled into the coffee lounge at the end of the barn, laughing, planning workshops for dressage and showjumping, gossiping. Didn't these people have homes to go to? It was no better in the morning, Mrs Beasley bustling round feeding everyone before the owls in the wood were abed or the blackbirds out of it. The next morning Sadie arrived to find a track trod round Teena's box and the excellent haylage in the rack untouched. The mare fidgeted horrendously when Sadie tried to put on her saddle and was downright naughty to ride; there was no communicating with her. She wasn't bucking or rearing, just fretting and running, sweating and swerving. It was such a lovely yard and close to where Sadie lived and the salon where she worked.

Surely the horse would settle? Please!

* * *

A week passed and if anything Teena was worse. Sadie was becoming familiar with the taste of the sand in the indoor school, so often had she fallen off. Everyone at the yard was sympathetic. Everyone had a theory about what Sadie should do. She daren't tell husband John about her. What would he say? All that money! Would, perhaps, Paddy take Teena back? Mrs Beasley caught the mare as Sadie had fallen off for the umpteenth time, on this occasion attempting a little Sunday morning ride out with others from the yard. This time she didn't lead her back to the barn – no, "Come, pet," she said and led her to the small yard behind her house.

Here was a collection of six old stone boxes, some store rooms and a garage. An ancient pony wandered loose along with a sheep, by the name of Basil, that had been a pet lamb but which had now grown to enormous proportions. Mrs Beasley's own steed, as sturdy as herself, a good plain bay, munched hay placidly in one of the stables. The turnout for this yard, unlike the immaculate post and rail for the main yard, was some poor grass surrounded by tall hedges. Around the stables it was spectacularly untidy, overgrown with nettle and elderberry and ivy wherever Basil couldn't reach it. There was a broken barrow stacked with broken automatic drinkers, bags of baler band, bags of bags. A cart overladen with muck from the boxes with a scuffy hen atop, scratching muck into the yard in her search for grubs. A mess, yes; a haven of peace and quiet, definitely.

Teena was led into a deeply strawed bed and her tack removed. She was sweating and excited but was too slow to rush out of the box before Mrs Beasley let her down. The stable door was shuffled shut and secured with its string and Teena was left to 'get over herself'. "Leave her be," said Mrs Beasley to a sore and shaken Sadie, "I'll do her up later, you go home and have a good long soak."

"I'm at my wits' end." Sadie was trying hard not to cry, though a tear escaped down her cheek.

"Now, love," Mrs Beasley rubbed Sadie's arm, "you come back tomorrow and we'll sort this together, mmm?"

After a long shift at the salon – pensioners' day, perms and blue rinses – Sadie did not feel like doing battle with a recalcitrant mare, so she was delighted that when she arrived at the yard to find Mr Beasley driving Teena in long reins.

"Halloo!" shouted Mr Beasley. "She had a bit of a turn at first, but she's settled down now."

Indeed, Teena was at that moment trotting in circles, one ear facing Mr Beasley, waiting for instruction. At last she looked the promising horse Sadie had purchased from Paddy Nolan.

"Shall I ride her today?" Mrs Beasley surprised Sadie by asking.

The large lady duly removed the lunge lines and side reins and led Teena to the mounting block. There was no walking Teena as Sadie would have done: Mrs Beasley booted her straight into trot round one end of the school, Wellington-booted feet stuck forward, bottom stuck out back. Teena was as good as gold. Sadie enjoyed watching them; she felt silly for not being able to manage Teena like that by herself.

With Mrs Beasley to help her, Sadie was soon riding Teena again. The mare stayed in the 'back yard' and was turned out with the bay cob, Topper, belonging to Mrs Beasley. The bay was an excellent lead horse, taking Teena and Sadie over the narrow wooden bridge over the beck or over the logs and hedges through the wood. Teena began to relax more and more, even to look forward to being ridden. Sadie had to make sure she was concentrating at work: there had been swathes of gentlemen's hair cut off to the scalp when she had forgotten the spacer, hair dyed the wrong colour, wrong styles embarked on, all when she was thinking what she would do with Teena later.

It was their first show when the penny really dropped for Teena. Just a little event at the yard but Sadie was as excited as a little girl going to her first gymkhana. Everyone from the yard tried to support this event which was followed by a barbecue. There were cars and dogs and children. People plaited manes and oiled hooves. There were some showing classes but Sadie didn't think Teena would be good either cantering around in a group or standing still. So she entered the combined training which was a simple dressage test followed by a course of show jumps. Teena loved it. 'Look at me!' said her proudly carried tail and sharp pricked ears. Teena and Sadie went around the jumps as if they were joined together. It seemed to Sadie that Teena was reading her mind, so light was she in her hand. She was delighted to be awarded second prize.

They went to more shows usually with someone from the yard. Teena and Sadie, a team. Over the months, many more rosettes joined the first ever second one proudly displayed in Sadie's tack store at the yard.

Sadie would follow a hard day on her feet at the salon with a ride or lesson on Teena. After a ride she loved to brush the sweat from Teena's soft coat, massaging her muscles with the brush. The two were great friends now. Today, as usual, she didn't hurry home, nattering to friends at the yard over a coffee; even so, John still wasn't home before her. She had made a lasagne but it would be well past its best by the time John saw it. Once again she ate alone, had a long hot shower and fell into bed. She had meant to read for a while but she was soon asleep. She woke and instinctively felt across the bed for John. He wasn't there. She looked at the clock. One a.m. Realising there was light from downstairs, she put on one of John's sweatshirts and went John-hunting. She found him with his laptop in the kitchen. "You're not still working, surely?" she asked.

"No, I'm shopping!" he smiled, swivelling the laptop for her to see.

Through sleepy eyes Sadie squinted at the screen, "Mountain bike? You're buying a mountain bike?"

John took Sadie's hand. He promised himself he would talk to her so... "Do you know," he started, "when I saw the picture of Teena in that scruffy stable I was cross, I thought she lived in a smart barn. And then you said she liked it better there. And then I was cross again. That horse, I thought, has more choice about its life than I do. And it–"

"She," interjected Sadie.

John waved a hand, "– Yeh, *she* sees far more of you than I do and –" And John told her how he felt old before his time and he felt fat and he hated his commute.

"So get another job," said Sadie, like it was that easy. But she wanted him home more so very much as well, aware that they were drifting apart.

She loved her life, their cosy home, loved her job at the salon. Her colleagues and clients were friends. And then there was Teena. Bringing her on had given Sadie such pleasure, a sense of achievement. And everyone at the yard so friendly. Of course she stayed chatting at the yard in the evening, why would she want to come back to an empty house?

John stuck by his resolution. He lost weight. He cycled himself fitter. He often cycled with Sadie and Teena on a Sunday along the miles of bridleways around Tang Hall, through the beautiful woods, where Teena enthusiastically popped over fallen logs. And he went with them both when they competed whenever he could. Teena continued to do well and Sadie couldn't be happier, so it was hard for her to look pleased when John announced he had found the perfect job in Leeds. Of course she had wanted him to find a more suitable job, she just thought it wouldn't mean any change for her. And of course she would support him; it was easy for her to find work and he was the main wage-earner by a very long way. At last, for him, an end to the dreadful commute. There was much to do. A house to sell, a house to buy, a new home to find for Teena, a new job for Sadie. But for Sadie the goodbyes came all too soon. Work colleagues and loyal customers of course, but most of all dear Mrs Beasley and all her friends at the yard, all of whom had been so kind and helpful to her.

Settling in a village just north of Leeds, Sadie had a choice of two yards for Teena near to home. Neither was perfect. Blackberry Farm had good old stone boxes and plenty of turnout but there was no school in which to work Teena. Six miles of bridle path away was a larger livery with wooden boxes and a school and decent turnout. The stables at Brockwell Park weren't as pleasant as Blackberry, but the school swung it for Sadie, even though here the yard was staffed by a sulky girl, Jenna, the owners concentrating on the farm. Blackberry was DIY, with the large Edith Fox at the helm. At Brockwell there was part livery, so someone would look after Teena when Sadie was at work. Teena was duly expensively transported to Brockwell to be received by Jenna. The lazy girl dragged Teena off the box and put her in her allocated stable, not bothering to remove her travel boots or head collar. She already had Sadie pigeonholed: posh rich bitch. Who did she think she was? That accent! Who says 'wHen' and 'wHere'? She determined not to like Sadie from the start. And now here was her posh horse delivered, a push button animal that just did as it was told. Any idiot could ride it; obviously, it was another expensive purchase to make Sadie look good. When Sadie arrived and found Teena with her boots still on, no hay in her rack, no water in her bucket, she simply asked Jenna where the hay and water were, so that she might fetch them herself.

"Here we go," said Jenna to herself, "Already pecking my head!" Over the next few days Jenna made sure her employers know Sadie was being awkward, a blatant lie, while doing everything she could to deprive and upset Teena. If

Sadie was unable to come in as she was working an evening at her new job in a Headingley salon, Teena was left without either food or water. Similarly she was left unfed if Jenna was responsible for her in the morning. Jenna turned Teena out last and bought her in first so she spent long hours in her stable. Often she was turned out with horses that Jenna knew would bully Teena and she would come in with kicks to her legs and bites to her neck. Her rug was never changed nor her feet picked out. Whenever possible Jenna delivered a blow to Teena's head or ribs with a fork or broom. Of course Sadie noticed the change in Teena: the glowing coat was now starey, the ribs showing as the weight fell away. How miserable Teena looked! Despite the soreness of the ulcers Teena had developed and the fact she was often hungry or thirsty, Teena continued to try her best for Sadie. If she said anything to Jenna the girl lied, saying Teena must be a fast eater. When she mentioned it to the yard owners they backed Jenna: she was a good girl, they said. Perhaps Sadie was mistaken? They gave the impression they thought her a liar. So Sadie took to keeping Teena's feeds at home in the garage and bringing them herself, standing over Teena as she ate. She always filled the hayrack and water and luckily Jenna was too lazy to sneak back and remove either. Jenna had her friends in the yard and a group of them were always huddled together, sniggering behind hands. If Sadie took Teena in the arena to school they were in immediately, putting up jumps and winging round on their own horses. If Sadie fetched out poles they were in to school and demanded she remove them. It gave great pleasure to Sadie and, indeed to Teena, to spend time brushing Teena's mane and tail. Polishing her coat. Oiling her hooves. Jenna clattered around outside as much as possible to spoil their quiet time, fetching out the leaf blower she used to clear the yard, running the strimmer.

Sadie had to hack Teena out on her own. No one seemed interested in showing her any routes, so she was pleased when John suggested he come out with them both on his bike one evening.

Just for a minute Sadie could imagine they were back at Mrs Beasley's, they had a lovely ride. When they returned John took the saddle back to the tack room where Jenna and a couple of mates were sprawled on the sagging armchairs below the saddle racks.

"Good evening, girls," said John. He didn't get a reply. As he left the room he heard Jenna's mocking echo, "Good evening, girls…" as plummy as she could manage, then the three lasses burst into laughter.

"Are they always like that?" he asked Sadie when he got back to the stable.

"'Fraid so, right little nest of vipers."

"Don't know why you put up with it. Just move Teena somewhere else. Hey, how about a drink at that funny little pub in the village?"

"Yeah, looks like it's ashamed of itself, doesn't it? Crouching in a corner behind the church!" Sadie finished brushing Teena and made sure she had plenty of hay and water. She kissed the velvet nose, right on the pink bit, with passion.

"Can I have one of those?" John puckered up and got a pony nut pushed between his lips. "EUGH," he spat the nut into his hand, scooped Sadie up by her waist and tried to force-feed her the nut. Laughing together, he and Sadie then left the Cayenne in the yard and walked hand in hand down to The Rams Head.

It was certainly an ancient build with a white pebble-dashed facade and red tiled roof.

John had to bend his head to get through the door and watch out for the beams once inside. The landlord didn't have the same problem, being five feet high and about the same wide. He didn't say anything to the pair as they walked in, merely acknowledging them with a lift of his head, a raise of his shaggy eyebrows.

"Pint of bitter and a white wine please," said John, leaning on the bar.

Sadie was taking in the decor, the smell of tobacco smoked into every beam and every wall for centuries. There were stuffed rams' heads all over the place, some obviously very old, mothy, goggle-eyed fell sheep, others newer, more modern breeds better stuffed. Behind the bar, directly below the optics displayed in a glass fronted oak box, was a heavy crucifix decorated with turquoise and amber. The landlord, Simon Bagford (Baggy), followed her gaze, his eyebrows dancing up and down his forehead. Baggy poured the pint, stopping to let it settle, leaning forward across the bar, eyebrows flying up his forehead.

"Ah, the crucifix! See these rams here?" He waved his hand around the pub lounge. "Sacrifices!" He nodded sternly and topped up the pint.

"Seriously?" asked Sadie, incredulous.

"Ooh, yes. It was said, yer see, that there was a monster, bigger than a bear, fiercer than a lion in that wood up the hill. Hellwood. Well, it had a preference for human flesh so every year the villagers here would sacrifice a lamb for it that it might leave their children alone and that they might have safe passage through the wood. Then every ten year they would leave it a ram, but, yer see, it never ate the ram's head."

He paused and reached for a wine glass, polished it with the glass cloth on the bar and fetched the wine, bottle in one hand, glass in the other he continued his story, eyes wide, eyebrows higher than ever.

"Then one evening this priest comes to this pub to water his horse and probably his self as well. But the villagers, you see, had only taken the ram up that afternoon and the priest was all for going up to the monastery before dark. That's Hazelbank, what's a hotel now. They warned him, but he would go, wouldn't he? Next morning the villagers went to pick up the ram's head but the sheep was still there on the path, tethered to its stake and next to it stood the priest's mare. All they found of him was this crucifix. Preference for human flesh, yeh see." Baggy nodded affirmation of his story as he tapped the case of the crucifix.

"Creepy," said Sadie. "My mare is always on edge going through there."

"Is she?" Baggy's eyebrows danced. "They know, ye see."

Sadie and John took their drinks and went to a table by the window just as a couple of old blokes walked in. "Can't sit there!" shouted one. "That's our seat. Dominoes," as if that explained everything.

Baggy didn't intervene. He was wiping the horns of his latest acquisition, a fine Dalesbred ram on an oak plack, beautifully preserved. What a pity, the taxidermist had said, that it didn't have more of a cape.

The pair took themselves to the snug, the little room behind the bar area. It was quiet in here, the only sound the steady, heavy tick of a long case clock. "Do you think the priest took off the crucifix to scare off the monster?" pondered Sadie

"Sadie, I don't think there was a monster. People were just scared of the forest back then."

"Sitting here though, well it's like being in a time warp. Seems easy to believe in a monster."

"Anyway, a monster wouldn't be scared of a crucifix, it's hungry, not evil. Speaking of which, what are we having tonight?"

They finished their drinks and wandered back to Brockwell for the car.

* * *

Finding her saddle slung on the floor Sadie finally decided she'd had enough. It was a Tuesday and she had a late start at work so there was time to ride early. The forecast was for storms and lashing rain and already the air was heavy, hot and humid. Sadie tacked Teena up and set off along the bridleway straight to Blackberry farm. It was a pleasant ride, though there were little challenges for a horse. You started up a hill to Hellwood. Here the bridleway cut through the Western end of the wood over the shoulder of the hill. And dark the wood was, thick with pine and conifer and bordered by brambles.

As always, Teena was on edge as she went through the shady tunnel the wood created over the path. The bridleway then dipped down through fields stocked with cattle and sheep behind sturdy hedges. After this, you passed Jackdaw Farm where there was a shop with a petting area – well, Teena didn't mind the two wallabies near the bridleway if they didn't jump about! The lane past Jackdaw crossed the bridleway and led to the village so you could ride a loop round, a mile along the bridleway then three more along the road. Occasionally the bridleway was used as a short cut by farm traffic. Shortly after there was an underpass beneath the main road where traffic roared overhead with the pass echoey, cool and damp. The path through arable then came to a gate, not one easy to open from a horse, especially when they were trying to be several hands taller than they actually were and snorting at the cattle on the other side! The exit from the field was over a narrow wooden bridge over a beck. *Clomp, clomp, clomp*, went Teena's hooves and she jumped off the bridge. Whatever lay ahead, Teena braved it for Sadie as she trusted her rider and felt the calm reassurance of leg and hand. Within 45 minutes of leaving Brockwell, Blackberry Farm was in sight.

Edith was throwing a ball for her terriers when Sadie and Teena arrived. She took in the handsome grey and tidy pilot. "Morning!" she trilled, "hope you haven't come far, the heavens are about to open."

Sadie was quietly wanting not to go back at all. Tense and anxious she explained her situation to Edith. She was so sorry she had picked Brockwell. Edith rubbed her chin, terriers jumping up her broad legs for the ball. She had had a couple of folks come to the farm from Brockwell. "We're full, really, but if I move my pony I can fit you in. Give me until the weekend, can you? Then I can sort turnout too."

"Thank you, thank you," Sadie sighed with relief. "See you Saturday, I'll ride over first thing and drive my gear over later." A few more pleasantries and Sadie was on her way home, happy to have arranged to go to Blackberry, in a hurry to get home before the storm. "Keen," thought Edith. But she knew all about Brockwell.

It was as if night were approaching it was so dark. Cloud bubbled ahead. Even the birds in the hedgerows were silent as they felt the approaching storm. Sadie nudged Teena into a trot; there was no time to waste. They swung up the last hill before Brockwell with less than half a mile to go, this is where the bridleway narrowed to the single track lane as it went through Hellwood, into the tree tunnel over the track. Sadie and Teena felt the strong draught of the haar before the storm, both wanted to be back before the storm broke.

Already thunder rumbled in the near distance. Then, as they reached the edge of the wood, Teena slammed to a halt. Her ears were pricked hard forward, her nostrils flared wide snorting, trying to catch scent. Every muscle in her body was tense.

"Hey girl, good girl, walk on."

Sadie stroked the rigid neck, she could feel Teena's heart hammering against her left calf. And then she could see movement. Something big, brown and lumbering at the edge of the wood. It was eating something; she could hear the crunch of bone even over the gathering wind. Before she could really get a fix on it, Teena had spun, Sadie staying in the saddle by the trained reflex of a lifetime's riding. Then Teena was bolting, forty miles an hour into the teeth of the storm. The sparks flew up from her flying hooves if she hit a stone. Now the rain thrashed down; lightning, then thunder rent the air. By the time Sadie could pull Teena up they were both soaked through, shaking with adrenaline and exertion. Sadie took the road to Brockwell and arrived back soaking wet, chilled to the bone and late for work.

Jenna was delighted by the state of the pair as they arrived, bedraggled, back. Sadie was shaking and Teena clearly on edge. "We had to go round by the road," said Sadie to Jenna as she untacked Teena in her stable out of the pouring rain, "there was something in the wood that really spooked Teena."

"OOOH! You see Baggy's monster, did you?" said Jenna, laughing out loud.

"It was a big, brown thing, crunching up bones..." described Sadie. *Here we go*, thought Jenna, *the posh horse has shied at a deer or dog or summat and the posh rider is cacking her knickers 'cos it wagged an ear. Pathetic.* She left Sadie to sort out Teena and went to catch up with Snapchat. Having rubbed

Teena down, Sadie went straight round to the farmhouse and told the owners, Roger and May Jenkins, she would be leaving first thing Saturday, never mind that she had paid another three weeks' livery. May offered tea; she wanted to know what had been going on, but Sadie was late enough for work already. She was keen to rug Teena and give her some time out despite the steadily falling rain.

As soon as Sadie was gone, May was round to Jenna. She had supported the girl every time a client had complained, after all staff were hard to come by, but here was the fourth person leaving in as many months. She gave Jenna a piece of her mind and no mistake. Jenna was fuming. Obviously posh pants had gone straight round the house and slanged her off. Well she'd give Sadie a proper send off, just you see!

The next evening saw Sadie walk up the hill around the back of Brockwell towards Hellwood. Up the gravelly track winding up between sturdy hedges. It was easier to see what was ahead from a horse than walking. Soon she came to the tree tunnel, Hellwood covering the hilltop and running down to a beck on one side and to a footpath to the village on the other. She climbed through tangled barbed wire fencing, past the old signs fallen to the bramble-covered floor and newly erected ones. 'PRIVATE' they said, and 'KEEP OUT'. She picked her way deeper into the wood. A jay scolded. Then just the soft peaceful sweep of the wind through the treetops, the lazy buzz of a fly. Further from the track there were fewer brambles and narrow deer tracks threaded their way through fallen branches and crowded saplings. Sadie had wanted to check the wood out before she came this way on Saturday, see if there was any sign of what had spooked Teena. But all was peaceful. She sighed and turned to leave and almost walked into an old man standing behind her, propping himself up with a thumbstick.

"Oh, oops, so sorry!" spluttered Sadie, "I mean, I know it's private, but something frightened us yesterday and I had to set my mind at rest."

"Ah!" nodded the old man and then, placing his hand on Sadie's arm, his touch warm and strong, "Be sure, there is nothing in this wood that will harm you or your beautiful horse."

"But how…?" started Sadie, but the old man was already walking away, making surprising speed as if he knew every deer track. And like the deer he soon vanished into the wood. Sadie felt confident they could take the bridleway on Saturday. Besides, John was coming with them on his bike.

As Sadie prepared to leave Brockwell, Jenna prepared her leaving surprise. Foraging around through piles of rags and boxes in the garage at home she at last found what she'd been looking for: the giant soft toy black panther she'd won at a fair some years ago. She knocked off a bit of excess dust and mould and polished the shiny green eyes. Now *here* was a monster! On Friday afternoon she was undisturbed as she walked from the village up the footpath to the hilltop wood. She lobbed Mr Panther over the wire and scrambled after him. Equipped with baler band and using branches the panther was positioned such that with a pull on the baler band it would be catapulted – 'leap' – up to the bridleway. It worked a treat! She could easily retreat to the footpath unseen.

As soon as Teena had eaten her feed on Saturday morning Sadie and John were preparing to leave. The Cayenne was packed with the last of Teena's gear and John would cycle back and fetch it. It was nearly seven when they left. Sadie was pleased Jenna was nowhere to be seen. Late again! The trio set off in the fresh still morning. Sadie was reassured John was with them, just like when they were at Tang Hall, chatting away. Even so, as they approached the wood Sadie felt Teena begin to tense, snuffing the air.

"Steady, steady..." soothed Sadie.

They turned the last bend into the arch of trees and *WHOOSH*! The panther landed on the wire. Teena spun and was off like a greyhound out of the traps; Sadie lost an iron but soon regained balance as they rocketed along downhill.

Meanwhile, Jamie Larson was late for work at Jackdaw Farm Shop again. He was supposed to see to all the pets before the shop and cafe opened at eight. As we know, the bridleway is two miles shorter than the road, so he had decided to take a short cut and race his Ford Ka up it. He was having a great time bouncing along the bridleway, headphones plugged in. Seeing a grey horse galloping flat out towards him as he turned a bend really caught him out, he just froze. Sadie was equally surprised. There was no way she could halt Teena's headlong charge and no space to pass the car. Instead she dug her heels into Teena's flanks. "Up!" she shouted. It was enough to focus Teena's attention: the question was asked and she answered it with all her heart and every fibre of her being, turning in an instant from a bolting horse back into the well-schooled animal she had become. She jumped her best ever jump up and over the little blue car. Jamie felt as if the whole thing happened in slow motion. He saw the horse soar over him, its hooves, the fluffy girth guard and belly, the slight 'clunk' as a trailing hind hoof caught the top of his windscreen. Sadie felt adrenaline burn across her chest. She could barely feel her hands. She nearly fell off as Teena pecked slightly on landing but, wow, here they were, alive. Teena was delighted with her own effort and put in a small buck. She pulled herself up to a walk. John saw Sadie and Teena disappear at speed and heard the crunch of car tyres on gravel. He also saw someone hurrying through the undergrowth towards the footpath. He went after his wife.

John stopped alongside Jamie, his car stalled, his eyes still on stalks. "It jumped the car," he said to John. Having established Jamie worked at Jackdaw and that everyone was in one piece he called a "See you later!" to Jamie and pedalled after Sadie. She had dismounted Teena and was checking her legs for injury. A small trickle of blood ran down her near hind hoof; the hair still stuck to the roof of the Ford. Still, it was a long way from her heart, as Mrs Beasley would have said and Teena wasn't lame on it.

Sadie really didn't want to go back to Brockwell. As John pulled alongside she asked "Do you think we can go on to Blackberry by the road? It's further but I think Teena is sound."

"Never mind her," says John," are *you* okay?"

By way of reply Sadie, smiling, placed her hand behind his neck, stood on tiptoes and kissed his lips. "C'mon let's go." And John pedalled off ahead.

At Jackdaw Jamie came out to greet them: there was, he said, a big bag of carrots for the wonder horse for Sadie to pick up whenever. Sadie felt ridiculously happy. She was leaving Brockwell. She had John. She had the bestest ever horse in the world. There was a friendly reception waiting at Blackberry. While John retraced his path to fetch the car, Sadie hosed the poorly hoof before Teena was turned out in a small paddock. Here she could see and sniff the horses she would be turned out with and there would be no fighting later.

Why ever had she gone to Brockwell?

That evening Mrs Sedgewick decided she would walk Spins, her spaniel, up the footpath to Hellwood and back down the bridleway to the village. A good strong walk this lovely summer evening. As she walked up the path she let Spins off the lead and he ran ahead of her, nose down snuff-snuffing, tail wagging, working out who had passed and when. He then caught a fresh exciting smell and pushed himself over the tangled verge into the wood. Mrs. Sedgewick lost sight of him.

"Spins! Spins! Where are you! C'mon!" she called and "Bloody dog!" under her breath.

Presently he emerged from the track a little further down, carrying something black and heavy-looking. As he came nearer, Mrs. Sedgewick could see he had picked up a boot. "Dead!" she commanded Spins, meaning him to leave it, but he carried it right to her, whining as he dropped it at her feet. She picked it up to throw it away but quickly realised why it had looked so heavy for Spins. The boot still contained a foot. She nearly saw a return of her breakfast and certainly felt light-headed. Hands shaking, she fissled her mobile out of her gilet pocket and managed to call the police.

Oh, yes, everyone was questioned and a team of police went through the wood with a fine-tooth comb. Blood was found, but it was that of a rabbit. A glove was found, but it belonged to an old man who took a great interest in the search while leaning on his thumbstick. Anyhow, he owned the wood so would often walk through. No, the foot was all of Jenna that was ever found.